THE GREEN MAN OF GRAYPEC

By
FESTUS PRAGNELL

I0616822

ARMCHAIR FICTION
PO Box 4369, Medford, Oregon   97501-0168

*For more information about Armchair Books and products, visit our
website at…*

www.armchairfiction.com

Or email us at…

armchairfiction@yahoo.com

STRANDED IN A FANTASTIC WORLD...

One minute Learoy Spofforth was a former American tennis champion, enjoying a visit to London with his lovely wife—the next minute he was a muscular savage on the weird world of Graypec, fighting for the possession a primitive but beautiful blonde.

Catapulted by a strange science into a universe existing within an atom, not knowing if he could ever return, Learoy finds himself involved in the greeds and lusts of primeval men and women at war with a crustacean form of life. Suspense builds through climax after climax to a finish that is as startling as the premise. This is the novel about which H. G. Wells said, "...I think it's a very good story, indeed, of the fantastic scientific type and I was much amused and pleased to find myself...in it."

CAST OF CHARACTERS

LEAROY SPOFFORTH
When he offered to help his brother with his discovery, he was sure it would only be for a few hours…but thirty years?

CHARLES SPOFFORTH
Inventing something spectacular only brought him grief with the press. What he needed was a volunteer to help prove his words!

KASTROVE
He had really 'gone ape' over a blonde he captured, but trying to help her could mean losing his life.

GRAWTOK
Cunning, deadly, and usually unchallenged—he wanted the new captive girl for himself, and was willing to kill to have her.

ISSA
Captured by the ape-men when her ship crashed, she found herself surrounded by lust and violence.

THE CHIEF
He had ruled with smoke and mirror tactics for quite some time— but now someone was asking too many questions!

THE LARBIES
These were the real rulers of Kilsona, strange mollusk-type creatures that had more power over the planet than any man.

CHAPTER ONE

(Statement of Learoy Spofforth, former lawn tennis champion of the U.S.A., taken in Old Bailey where the said Learoy Spofforth is awaiting trial for murder.)

I HEREBY DECLARE THAT THIS STATEMENT IS MADE ENTIRELY of my own free will, that no threats or promises have been made to induce me to confess and, in particular, that I have not been subjected to any severe questioning by the police.

I am soon to be charged with the murder of Charles Spofforth—my brother. They say they caught me, with the bloodstained weight in my hand, still pounding away at the bloody mess that had once been my brother's head—that it took four strong men to pull me away from the corpse. They are so sure of everything that they haven't even bothered to question me since that first moment when they brought me in, with my brother's blood still fresh on my hands.

If what they say is true—and I must believe them since I have no memory of my first return to this world—then it is beyond understanding for I loved my brother. Even during those long years—which were only minutes to him—when I felt that he had doomed me to an impossible life.

Last week I visited my brother, thirty long years ago— thirty long years that passed in a single day! And those years were more than twice as long as the years we are accustomed to. My birth was 28 years ago, yet I am more than 88 years old—half of me, that is; the other half is dead, and if still alive would be thousands of years of age.

I am even uncertain as to who I really am. My name is Learoy Spofforth, a name well known to the people of my country and abroad. Only last year I won the American championship at lawn tennis for the second time, and this year I captured the English championship at Wimbledon also. Soon after the tumultuous reception that greeted the victorious American team, I called on Charlie, my brother. He was greatly changed from what he had been when I had last seen him several years before. Then he had been rather plump with full, round cheeks and thickish lips, a careless, cheerful manner; but now he was hard and lean; his cheeks were sunken and his lips were thin, tight lines. But in his eyes was the greatest change; they had an air of being wider open, intense and full of fire. It was not until I had been with him for some time that I noticed that he was growing bald.

I kidded him about his thinness, remarking that he looked as if he also had been in hard training for tennis playing.

"Brain work, Lea", he answered, laughing, "gets a man down if he overdoes it, you know. My doctor made me take a rest. He seemed to think I was getting too seriously involved in a quarrel over my latest discovery."

We were dining at Charlie's home at the time, and my wife was deep in conversation, about dresses, I believe, with the quiet little woman who was Charlie's wife.

I nodded. "I saw the reports in the papers of your discovery. 'American scientist invents microscope to see atom', they said. 'Declares there are men on atoms. Hopes to establish communication'. Whole columns of it. Then the next day umpteen scientific Johnnies were writing to say that it was all wrong, and that some of your results were probably faked. Tell me about it."

Charlie's brow clouded. "Jealousy", he said. "One meets with it even in our scientific world, especially when an unknown man hits on something really extraordinary. I blame the papers chiefly, though; they seized on the sensational part of my work and made the most of it—took hardly any notice of my microscope at all until I was foolish enough to drop a hint about finding living creatures on atoms, and then they were full of it. I couldn't say a word without it being twisted around to mean something else. I can tell you I soon began to wish I had said nothing about men on atoms."

"Has it harmed your reputation?" I asked, sympathetically.

"Has it!" he exclaimed with bitterness. "No one will pay any serious attention to what I say now. I am the man who tried to get a lot of cheap publicity by broadcasting mad stories of what he could do—the man who brought science into disrepute!"

"But there is some solid foundation behind all these stories, I suppose? Something you could prove and make them admit it?" I asked.

"That's just it," he exclaimed so loudly that my wife looked around at us. "It's all true, every word of it—every word the paper said, yes, and more!"

I took a sip of port and tried to collect my thoughts. I wondered what was the most tactful way to meet such a suggestion.

"Every discovery has had to fight against prejudice at first," I tried. "If you can prove your words—" Platitudes I know, but it was all I could say.

"Would you help me?" he asked, sharply.

"But what could I do? I am no scientist."

"That doesn't matter. Will you join me tomorrow and take part in an experiment to prove to the world that I am telling the truth? I need somebody, and it would not really be fair to ask, say, a gardener; it may be too dangerous. Besides, I must have somebody to whom people will listen."

At this point he broke off, seeing that my wife was listening, and we began to talk about something else, leaving his question unanswered.

After dinner he asked me to follow him and led me into another room. I expected to see his laboratory, but there was nothing suggestive of experiments here, and we went through the open French windows onto the lawn. From here we followed a gravel path through the grounds until we came to a very new long brick building. It was at the back of the house and well hidden away, in view of its size, for I think it covered more ground than the house itself.

One end of this great barn had been used by gardeners as a repository for flowerpots, spades, plants, and the like. In the center of the building was a machine that looked to me like one of those rotary printing presses that turn out our daily newspapers, but without the white rolls of paper. It took up most of the space.

"What do you think of my microscope?" asked Charlie.

"Where is it?"

"That's it, in front of you."

I gasped, for "that" was this huge affair, about five times the size of a streetcar.

"Why do you want so much water?" I asked, as I tripped over a leaden supply pipe four inches through.

"That's not water; that's my power cable. You see we have a very difficult thing to do; we have to magnify and amplify light and alter the wavelength all at the same time and without distortion. It is because everyone thinks it impossible to do so that they won't believe me. My system is in its infancy as yet, and extremely wasteful of power, but it works, as you'll see. Here," he pointed to two armchairs with black linen boxes in the seats, "is where the observers sit and see what is going on, on the atoms. Those boxes fit over their heads."

For the first time, I began to believe that my brother did know what he was talking about. This thing was too involved and costly to have been built in support of an illusion. The least I could do would be to help him justify himself.

"By all means, I'll help you," I said, "providing that it's not necessary for me to learn to operate this colossus. You know I never could study anything. What is this little machine at the back of my chair?"

"Oh, you'll learn what that is for quickly enough. Let's go back into the house. I don't believe in night duty. We'll go to work tomorrow."

"Good," I said. As I followed him back to the house, I was beginning to look forward to helping him—not realizing the form my help was going to take.

"Been showing Learoy over your old laboratory?" demanded Charlie's little brown-haired wife when we found the two women in the drawing room.

"We've had a look at the microscope," he admitted.

"There you are", she exclaimed to Mary, "as I told you. This is what I have to put up with; Charlie spends all of his time poking about there, and it's the hardest job in the world to drag him away, even when I throw a party. Don't you let him persuade Learoy to bury himself there too."

"No fear of that", said Mary, laughing, "my husband never could stick to one thing long, unless it was tennis. Why, when I was teaching him golf—"

"Woman", I said, severely, "there are hidden depths in my nature that even you do not suspect!"

"You've got to show me! But what is this I've been reading, Charlie, about your finding men and women on atoms? I always thought atoms were much too small."

I resigned myself to what I had been trying to dodge, a scientific lecture, but as a matter of fact, Charlie could put things so simply that anybody could follow him.

"It's no new idea, really. When atoms were first described, people noticed how like they were to little solar systems, small bodies whirling around a central sun; but the quantum theory and relativity and a lot of other things have shown atoms to be such complicated affairs that those older ideas were given up. An atom became a sort of dance of protons and electrons; but my microscope has added such a lot to those ideas that the orthodox scientists refused to accept it.

"Can you imagine our sun to be a mass of protons all fused together, in which mass the sunspots are disrupted electrons? While out in space electrons whirl around it like great electric storms? While this earth is part of a proton that accidentally got torn to pieces?"

"No", said Mary, "I can't say that I can imagine that, not unless I had plenty of time to think it over."

"Well, anyway, that is what my microscope shows me."

"Oh, Charlie, can we all see? It must be fascinating."

"I certainly have seen some very peculiar things, and I have also seen some horrible ones. But I wouldn't care to ask you to come and make observations with me; my machine is far from perfect yet, and it sometimes takes hours to get it adjusted so that atoms can be seen. One day I'll fix up a relay with a television screen in the drawing room, so that you can be playing bridge and when I find something particularly interesting, I'll ring a bell, put out the lights, and throw it on the screen." He smiled at my wife.

"But why can't I see now?" she asked. "Learoy is going to."

She must have guessed. Charlie gave me a quick glance and explained that I was only going to watch him work for an hour or so tomorrow.

"Tomorrow! But the Polkinhornes!"

It was an engagement I had forgotten.

"Oh, tell them I'm unwell," I said. I was rather amused at myself. I was beginning to feel as though I were on the verge of a big adventure and it was the first time I had ever put gazing into a microscope in that category.

The conversation turned to other subjects and a couple of hours later, Mary and I went home.

CHAPTER TWO

EARLY THE NEXT MORNING THERE WAS A TAP ON MY DOOR and a housemaid informed me that Mr. Charles Spofforth had rung up to ask what time he was to expect me. I sighed and told the girl I'd take the call in my bedroom.

"What do you want at this ridiculous hour?" I asked him, when I picked up the receiver.

"I've been ready and waiting for you for over an hour," Charlie responded.

"Good Heavens, man! Have a little consideration for the aged and infirm! Don't you go to bed at all? All right, I'll be along as soon as I can."

It was an hour later when I arrived at Charlie's house and he immediately led the way toward the laboratory. Arriving at the barn, we found a man in greasy blue clothes fussing about on a sort of platform on the microscope, at the top of an iron staircase that bore the words *Danger! High Tension.* Several electric motors were humming and sparking away, and lamps gleamed away in the mysterious recesses of the machine.

"All set, sir!" said the mechanic, hearing our steps. He did not look around.

"Well, keep it so," said Charlie. "We are depending on you absolutely today. I may not have another chance to speak to you, and any failure on your part may be more serious than you imagine."

The mechanic made a noise of injured dignity.

Charlie and I took our places in the armchairs. I was surprised to observe that he was trembling with excitement.

"See this?" he asked, indicating the machine I had inquired about the day before. "Know what it is?"

"Am I likely to know what it is?"

"It's a memory transferer."

"Uh—huh?"

"When we locate a man on the atom, I shall close this switch, and immediately all his memories will be transferred to you!"

"Eh, that's a weird sort of thing to do to your only brother. Why should you want to?"

"You're not afraid, are you? It's what I wanted you for. Our memories are independent of our material bodies, and don't you see that you will obtain, in a flash, everything there is to be known about the atom and living conditions on it? The greatest experiment ever made!"

"All right; I'm in your hands. Proceed. But I shall breathe more freely when it's all over."

Science lately has taken such strides that it all seems to me more like black magic than anything else, and there was a gleam in Charlie's eyes that I did not like. For a moment, I wasn't sure I wanted to help him—but I had promised, so I said nothing.

He fitted so many contrivances over my head and shoulders that I was almost afraid to move for fear of breaking something. Under that black cover, of course, it was quite dark.

"We're off," he said. "Watch carefully!"

In a sea of inky blackness a number of pinpoints of light of varying brightness stared at me like stars.

"Nuclei of atoms, shining by their own light!" His voice held a note of awe.

It was just this sort of view that one might see any clear night. The constellations were all strange, of course, and the starry specks stood out with exceptional sharpness against a sky of intense black.

After about ten minutes of this unchanging view, I asked Charlie when he was going to increase the magnifying power and bring them a bit closer.

"Doing all I can," he answered. "This is the tedious part of the business, finding individual atoms. At the present moment we are racing across the sub-microscopic sky at a terrific speed. Do you see one star getting brighter than the others? Watch it carefully."

It was a bluish body, and picked itself out of that starry background to rush upon us with menacing speed, swelling and growing brighter as it did so.

Have you ever stared out of the window of a moving train until it seemed that the train was still and the ground poured past you? I felt something like that now, as though the whole laboratory, Charlie's machine and my chair had melted away to nothing, and I was some ethereal being floating in a vast abyss of space, among those brilliant bodies. I forgot how small they really were and how huge I was in comparison; and when Charlie spoke his voice was that of some all-powerful entity, booming and reverberating through unthinkable distances.

That great blue sun swerved in its course and passed on the right. Then I waited again until another blue star rushed upon us, swelling to great size, then passed as the other had.

"No planets to either of those," observed my companion. "I think we may have better luck with this one. Its yellower color shows that it is not quite so hot."

Steadily the chosen star came on until it appeared much as our own sun does to us, and one could not look straight at it. Around it flared a huge and glorious corona such as men on earth can see only during a total eclipse. As Charlie hunted for planets that might be the abode of life, the sun began to dance about, to travel in erratic spirals and to disappear on the left, reappearing on the right.

This business of searching for planets proved a more tedious business than even the hunt for likely looking stars. Planets were dark bodies when we got on the wrong side of them, and even when we saw them, we couldn't tell them from the stars in the background until they were very close. Planets we found, but they were either too hot or too cold, and at least an hour passed before Charlie found the characteristic crescent shape that proved to be the body we sought.

CHAPTER THREE

THE SUDDEN RUSH AS WE PLUNGED AFTER THIS NEW PLANET made me tense all my muscles and grip savagely on the arms of my chair. So unprepared was I that it was not until afterwards that I realized that the movement was entirely illusory, and felt rather foolish about my momentary start.

As we approached this world, which I was later to know so well as Kilsona, or Graypec, it somehow seemed to get beneath us, and we dropped down towards it as though we were falling out of the sky. Below us was a sea of curling, white-topped waves that beat angrily on chalky cliffs.

"I wish you wouldn't do it!" I exclaimed, sharply.

"Do what?" he asked in pained surprise, but I heard him chuckle.

"Move the thing so fast. I keep forgetting it isn't us that's moving. For a moment I thought I was going to be drowned in that sea or smashed on those cliffs!"

Excitedly, he laughed, a laugh that had a note of triumph in it. "Think of the thrills you're getting! Why, if you were paying good money to be excited, you'd think it an excellent show."

Without further remark, we left that stormy sea and sped over a wide landscape. It was as though those dreams one has of flying freely through the air, more effortlessly than a bird, had come true. We swept over that changing landscape, sometimes at terrific speed, sometimes slowly to examine something that caught Charlie's eye. Around us were fleecy white clouds and below were extensive green prairies, sandy deserts, brown forests, and snowcapped mountain ranges. Charlie was looking for towns, airplanes, roads, railroads, or any other signs of human habitation, but he found none. Animal life there was in plenty.

We hovered over what seemed a fertile place, a wide plain bounded in one direction by hills through a gap in which flowed a river. As I looked, I thought Charlie had chosen well; if there were any men here they would be sure to come to this well-favored spot.

Now a painful flickering of the scene began to hurt my eyes; there it all was, pleasant and luxurious, apparently in late spring, with green grass, golden-brown woods, and yellow cattle; then—flash!—the river was in flood, cattle gone, grass withered, and great areas of forest burnt and black—flash!—and the river was ice, and leafless trees held up their black stems above a carpet of snow.

"The sudden changes", explained Charlie, "are due to the difference between time as we perceive it and as it is understood down there. Years there are little more than seconds to us. My machine takes a view like a snapshot, holds it a while, then takes another. Ah, that was a man then. Dash it, I was so busy talking that I missed the opportunity of making the transference. Be ready for it, because I shan't have time to warn you."

Indeed, quite a presentable man had appeared, walking swiftly across the plain, clothed in a sort of pink bathing suit with what might have been a bow and a quiver of arrows on his back. I often wonder if some sixth sense warned him of the danger he so narrowly escaped of having his thoughts, his very soul snatched out of his brain, and did he flee in sudden terror from that place? With our next view, he was gone.

Until now I had not thought seriously about Charlie's wild talk about transferring memories. First let him show me a man on the atom, then let him talk about wild things like that; but now the atom with the man on it was indisputably before me.

Charlie had accomplished what I thought impossible; might there not be something in that other mad project of his?—or had his incredible accomplishments gone to his head? And supposing Charlie to be right, what would it be like to have another man's thoughts suddenly injected into my brain?

With the fateful moment hanging over my head, I found myself waiting with a sort of sick apprehension, and hoping the man we sought would not appear.

A silvery yellow airplane—it was obviously that in spite of its unfamiliar form—lay wrecked on the grass, and nearer to me a man lying on his face had raised himself on his elbows to peer at it through the branches of a shrub. I noted that his body was muscular, without clothing, and covered with green hair, and that his arms were very long and his legs very short. In fact, though I call him a man, it would have described him almost as well to say that he was a green ape—a creature half man and half brute, like our own remote ancestors of prehistoric days. All these details I noticed in the brief second before I blacked out.

I think I screamed, for it seemed as though an explosion took place in my head, a great burst of light, a swirling as in a maelstrom, and I had a sensation of being sucked through a small opening, like water going through the waste pipe of a bath. For long minutes I hung in an empty space where there was no light, no sound, no sensation; all was formless and vague. At last I opened my eyes.

I was lying on my face on sandy soil and peering through a strange bush at a wrecked yellow flying machine.

No longer was I merely looking at an atom; I was actually on the atom, on a speck of matter so small as to be invisible under ordinary conditions. I was on the atom, in the body of an ape-man, while the savage was in the laboratory in my body! Yet I only partially realized this— part of my brain fought against the recognition of what had happened.

I heard, long after, from Charlie's own lips, a brief account of what happened in the shed after he pressed the switch. At the same moment, he took off his viewing box and turned on the light, for he was nervous of the results of his action. Hearing my cry, he jumped up and snatched the apparatus from my head. There was, of course, no apparent change in me, but when he looked into my eyes, Charlie knew that something was wrong; for those eyes stared at him in a dull, animal, bewildered fashion, like the eyes of an utter stranger, and without intelligence. For the first time, I think, my brother ceased to be a scientist and realized what he had done. He had condemned me to the body of a savage who might grow old and die before he could adjust his microscope.

At that moment the savage, who had been crouching in the chair with terror in his eyes, leaped at Charlie and swung a fierce blow at his face; but the blow was wild, and Charlie, easily avoiding it, knocked the brute unconscious and clapped the box over his head again, setting at once to work to bring back my proper personality from the atom.

Meanwhile, I was a new inhabitant of the world of Kilsona, and had first to accustom myself to my new surroundings. Thus, when I found myself lying on that hard, uneven ground, I became aware of a gnawing hunger in my stomach and felt a cold wind beating upon my body.

An explosion occurred on the grass to my left—such a queer thing, an explosion on the ground with nothing to cause it. It left a considerable hole and a puff of sulphurous smoke. The pain of the small fragments that struck me came a moment later. Another explosion occurred to my right, and with it came a hazy, bewildered realization that somebody was shooting at me. The shots were coming from the plane.

Near my left hand was an object very like a revolver with a short barrel. It looked heavy, but to the powerful muscles I now possessed it was but a trifle. Pressing the button that seemed to do duty for a trigger, I was surprised at a small cloud of blue smoke that sprang into being near the point I aimed at. Apparently, then, the man or animal whose body I had taken was in the act of carrying on a sort of private war with the occupants of the wrecked machine, and I had landed in the middle of it.

Just then a cry rang out, or rather, a roar. While it was not remarkably loud, not even as loud as I could shout at my loudest, it was very deep and harsh. Its note was below the range of the deepest human bass voice, while its harshness was a quality to set one's teeth on edge and make one sweat with fear. For it was obviously a war cry designed to express violent passions and to fill a foe with terror. At once it was answered by what I took to be an echo, with another and another till dozens sounded at last, seeming to come from scattered shrubs all about me. That landscape, seemingly deserted, was yet teeming with vindictive life.

"Korsho gah!" The cry was quite close to me and distinct from the other sounds, as though someone had asked a question. I turned my head to see a green ape-man, much like myself, hiding behind a bush and watching me. Looking around I saw many such figures, all with heads pointing towards the glassy yellow flyer.

"Korsho gah?" The speaker sounded impatient. That was not the actual sound, but is as near as I can express it. I knew now that it was addressed to me.

Somehow the words struck a cord in my memory, for Charlie's machine for transferring personalities is not perfect; it left fragments of the old personality behind. Thus the ideas of the caveman were present in my mind as a sort of dim background, vague memories to which I must trust if I were to live through the dangers of this strange world. That cry, "Korsho gah?" meant, "Are you hurt?"

It was a relief to know that I already had a friend, anyway. I barked back a word that sprang into my mind as meaning "no" in the language of the savages, and tried to follow it with a short, confident laugh. What I actually did was to emit a timid little war cry of my own.

Immediately afterwards I must have caused my new-found friend to doubt my word, for I dropped my head on my arms in an effort to concentrate on the remains of the ape-man's memory, so as to find out what was happening here, and why. That glassy yellow ship must hold the key to the problem.

Cautiously I peered at it. It was almost as transparent as glass. In fact, if it had been in the air, I should probably not have noticed it at all. The denser parts had a peculiar yellow sheen. It was not very large, perhaps twenty feet long and six from the ground to the upper deck; its cross--section was the shape of a hexagon. The upward tilt of its prow and stern made it very suggestive of a banana. It had short, broad wings, propellers and rudder, and one could pick out the outlines of engines and other opaque objects within. It had apparently landed heavily on its nose, the front parts being shoved in, but the boggy nature of the ground had saved it from becoming a complete wreck.

As I watched, a sort of door opened, and the savage cries broke out again as a woman ran onto the deck—and such a woman! Her slim figure had no trace of brutishness but might almost have belonged to any graceful, cultured woman of our own world, except that it was perhaps *too* thin and delicate. But for all her civilized form, she presented a strange enough figure as she ran out onto the deck of the damaged vessel. She had orange-yellow hair. Even at the distance, I could see this was its natural color. Her eyes were big and round, with heavy lashes and penciled brows. Her nose was very small and of perfect shape, a remark that also applied to her slightly full and *blue*-painted lips. Blue paint had also been applied to her cheeks and breasts, so that she gave the impression of having been shaped and painted according to a rather childish idea of beauty. For clothing, she wore a small red garment around her waist and hips and sandals on her feet. It was a picture of savage beauty, which stirred me as nothing ever, had before.

CHAPTER FOUR

MOST OF THE DETAILS I HAVE GIVEN OF THE APPEARANCE OF the woman, Issa, were visible the first time I looked at her, but others I have added from later knowledge. Now the sight of her affected me strangely. I found myself possessed of but one idea—I wanted her.

A haze of blue smoke surrounded the wrecked flyer, blue smoke that was the same as I had produced when I tested the weapon in my hand. It was to get above this smoke that she had exposed herself so recklessly, and stood now on the very highest point of the stern, outlined against the glow of the sky. Blue puffs appeared in the air about her and settled down to join the cloud that now nearly reached to her feet.

How was I to help her? To get up and run forward would be madness; she would kill me with her explosive bullets before I got halfway. The obvious plan was to turn my weapon on the others around me (I had found a switch that caused my pistol to produce explosive pellets), but not only did my soul revolt from such a series of cowardly murders, but also reason told me that it would simply be suicide and would not help her at all.

Somehow I must get to her, offer her assistance. But the ground near the vessel was bare of cover, or else the ape-men would already have taken advantage of it. The only means of getting closer to her was by the river, which flowed between high banks to within a hundred feet of the damaged nose of the ship. If I could get to that stream, swim under cover of the land, I could crawl out on the edge of that patch of marsh, and then it might not prove impossible to run the last little bit and get on the ship by means of the nose, which was embedded in the ground.

The same plan had occurred to others, for an ape-man slid noiselessly into the water and swam, as a dog swims, towards the woman. I could follow his progress under the water, never once coming up for air, until he crept cautiously out and joined a group of his fellows, sheltering behind a low mound quite close to the vessel. There were about eight of them, and the woman, her back to them, seemed wholly unconscious of them.

Hesitating now no longer, I jumped up and ran. "What a shock it was to find myself, instead of my accustomed five foot ten, little over five feet tall, due to my squat body and short legs, and my hardest efforts at running carrying me at not much more than a brisk walking pace over the ground!

Setting my teeth against the shock of the cold, I plunged into the clear, deep water in the middle of the stream. I struck out confidently in my usual swimming stroke, for I am a strong swimmer, thanks to Mary, my wife, but today I found myself unusually awkward. Instead of the arms and legs of Learoy Spofforth, I had the limbs of an ape-man, and when I attempted to swim in the frog-like fashion of a human being, those unaccustomed limbs betrayed me. In spite of the powerful muscles, I soon found myself sinking—in actual danger, in fact, of drowning. Soon I could no longer keep my head above water; the long weeds at the bottom wrapped themselves around my legs, and I gave myself up for lost.

It was then that I began to find out the unusual powers of this brute-like body of mine, for as I realized the use-lessness of struggling and let myself sink, being dragged through the weeds by the steady current, I was not in any distress for want of air, did not even want to breathe. It was long afterwards that I found out the reason for this. In that flat world with its frequent floods, nature had adapted all creatures to avoid death by drowning, nearly every land-animal having two capacious bladders of pure oxygen near the lungs.

My eyes were open, and I saw a thing like a foot-long gray lizard rushing to attack me. Instinct saved my life, for

I promptly flashed out an arm and caught him by the back of his neck in a grip that, to my surprise, crushed him. It was well that I did, for his bite would have been as deadly as that of a cobra.

Wondering why I had not thought of it before, I began to swim as a dog swims. At once I tore loose from the weeds and forged ahead through the water—almost as completely master of the water as though I had been a fish. A few moments later saw me crawling out of the stream, trailing long stems of weed, to join my fellow ape-men behind the mound. My gun was lost somewhere at the bottom of the river.

The semi-naked girl on the yellow ship seemed still ignorant of our presence there behind her; the blue gas was now over her head, but she took no notice of it, a fact at which I wondered until it occurred to me that she could probably hold her breath for long periods, the same as I could. The time seemed ripe for a dash, for once the ship was gained, there was a convenient rope by means of which one could hoist oneself on board. To get there I should have to run across a patch of swamp in which pools of water, coated with red scum, alternated with clumps of grass or shrubbery. There were snakes, lizards, and an anthill many feet high, as well as many other insects and reptiles.

If I stopped to think about danger, I should not have nerve enough to make that dash. Accordingly, I set my teeth and jumped up and ran. How was I to know I was practically committing suicide? I had picked out a route across firm patches that seemed to offer security from sinking in the slime.

I was on a strange world, and a world full of dangers of which as yet I knew nothing. Our world, this earth, is a very safe world; many generations of men have fought and millions have died to make it so. In some places men may have to beware poisonous snakes, tigers, bears, and the like, but these dangers are few, limited to certain places, and the dangerous animals are usually timid and of low intelligence—so that I gave the swarming life of that swamp scarcely a thought in making that dash. As I sprang forward, standing almost upright, yet going on all fours, so short were my legs and so long my arms, I became aware of an activity among the snakes, of a stirring among the ants. Another lizard struck at me but missed.

Instinct warned me of danger. I was aware of it as an uncontrollable spasm of terror that set me racing my hardest for the comparative safety of the ship. Like something forgotten and remembered I knew that all these myriad things were dangerous, most of them poisonous; some could even squirt poison out of their mouths with such force as to pierce the skin several feet away. The majority were vindictive, and all had some measure of intelligence. And I was invading their domain, trampling on their homes! The reason why the girl on the wreck had not even troubled to consider the possibility of an attack from behind was now only too painfully clear to me.

Looking back on that mad rush, I am forced to conclude that the only thing that saved my life, in spite of several attacks, was the fact that the air of the swamp was already polluted with the stupefying gas with which the ape-men were attacking the girl, the wind blowing from the ship in this direction and carrying wisps and streamers of gas with it; this may have rendered the reptiles slow and torpid of movement.

The rope looked thinner than I thought, but I had to trust to it. Throwing my weight on it, I pulled myself up; I pulled myself up, calling as I did so words that came into my head as meaning, "I come to help you."

It would have been better if I had said nothing. How, under the circumstances, could I expect her to believe me? I was to her one of the enemy, and as soon as my head appeared, she fired point-blank at it. In the same position, I myself would have expected treachery and done the same.

Again I escaped only because of the blue gas, which had now so nearly overcome her that her hand wavered, and the tiny but shattering missile missed me, but still was so close that I was all but stunned by the force of the explosion. Dazed, I lurched to my feet and rushed at her before she could fire again. At the last moment I remembered that the normal grip of my arms would break her fragile bones, and pushed the weapon aside instead of seizing her wrist.

Dropping the gun, she ran down the sloping deck past me towards the prow of the ship. In instant dismay I understood; thinking herself captured, she was going to throw herself to death among the ants, lizards, and scorpions of the swamp! She had courage, real courage, that girl whom I had thought a savage. I jumped after her, and pulled her back to safety without gripping her. I felt her warm flesh and the silky texture of the red garment around her hips. Turning wildly, she beat upon me with her bare fists. And strangest of all, she was winning that weird fight; for, in the moment when I saw her rush for the fore part of the vessel and knew her purpose, I had gasped with dismay, and in gasping I had forgotten to hold my breath, but had drawn that stupefying gas deep into my lungs. My head seemed to swell to a huge size, and all things about me began to grow misty and faint.

Fantastically, there appeared in the air before me an ape-man with a wide grin on his features. He landed on the deck with a plop, and forthwith others appeared beside him to gather around the girl—now lying unconscious on the deck—and growled deep with excited conversation that, to my surprise, I understood. Seeing me get aboard and struggle with their victim, they thought the battle won, and forthwith came charging out of their hiding places. My attempted rescue had been a signal for a general assault!

Had I been capable of doing so, I might have stood and fought from sheer humiliation when my brain had sorted out my surroundings and I knew what had happened. I might have struggled to death in defending beauty against brutal force, and in so doing have left beauty to her fate. I did strike hazily at one, but my dizzy blow was so ineffective that he did not even look around.

There were no questions asked. The ape-men had caught their quarry, and now all they wanted to do was to get away from their own blue gas as soon as they could. The girl was seized by her wrists and ankles and hurled over the side of the vessel; watching her fall, I saw her neatly caught by others on the ground, who began to carry her away.

One of the ape-men was gruffly asking whether I was capable of getting down and walking without assistance. His interest in me seemed strangely out of place, and it also annoyed me. As a matter of fact, the kindly solicitude these monsters sometimes showed to each other was one of the few marks they retained of their human ancestry; they were not so thoughtful for the other half of the race of mankind on Kilsona, of whom the captured woman was an example. Of the two branches it was hard to say which had sunk the lower—Issa's people or the green ape-men.

I refused his aid, fought to pull my reeling senses together, threw myself over the side in imitation of their easy leaps, landed awkwardly, and set off after the main crowd in a clumsy attempt to copy their swinging pivotal strides. It was a strong, healthy body I possessed, that of a male not quite full grown. When I became accustomed to this peculiar method of travel, I soon found myself catching up with the main body. One heavily built fellow seemed to be looking for someone, for he threaded his way through the others, then, seeing me, he growled, angrily.

"Blasted young fool! Ought to have your head bashed in."

For a moment I was surprised, uncertain whether to submit to this bullying or not, then my blood rose and I growled in answer:

"Perhaps *you* would like to bash it in?"

"That I would, you young devil!" he shouted.

It seemed to me that all the others were watching to see how I behaved in this crisis, that if I submitted I should become the butt of numerous bullies. Accordingly I swung at him a furious blow.

With astonishing agility he swerved and avoided my stroke. It was well for him that he did, for the power of the blow would have probably crushed his head.

"Kastrove," he exclaimed, "would you strike your own father?"

Kastrove was my name. I now recognized the man who spoke as the same as he who asked whether I was hurt when the girl fired at me, and who had offered to help me away from the wreck. The possibility that Kastrove might have friends or relatives here had not occurred to me. At once I saw that here was someone who, handled carefully, might be very helpful to me while I was on Kilsona.

Probably he would show me my way about, and help me avoid running unwittingly into danger, perhaps show me the best way to set about rescuing the captive girl.

I mumbled an apology for the attempted blow.

"All right," he said, freely enough, "but your hasty ways will get you killed before your time. Never did I see anything so mad as your rush across that deadly marsh, or your single-handed attack on the ship that the best warriors of Graypec were afraid to approach. Where's your gun?"

At that I remembered the strange weapon that produced the puffs of blue gas, now at the bottom of the river.

"Lost it," he scolded, "and carrying it today for the first time! How can you expect to be made a hunter and a warrior when you can't even look after your gun? Someone will have to stay with you and look after you. I don't know what the sub-chiefs will say."

He gave me a sharp, penetrating glance. "I suppose you wanted that yellow-haired woman from Teth-Shorgo for yourself? Mad young fool, you should leave such to older men; at your age the women of your own tribe should be good enough for you. I could point out several who would be willing to come into our cave if you were not so full of conceit. Still, you caught her, and none can deny your right to her. If it wasn't for this business of losing your gun, I don't know how that will affect it."

I pricked up my ears at that. Had I unintentionally won a right to the girl? I was torn by conflicting feelings. I wanted to remain faithful to Mary, but in that brief moment when I had held the struggling girl in my arms I had been aware of a passionate desire for her. My wife seemed a far off, distant person.

"Then she is mine?" I asked.

Throwing me a scornful glance, he replied: "After you, the only one of my ten sons still living, have risked losing your life and breaking your old father's heart, you pretend you don't know of the right you gambled for. Certainly she is yours, for one day only. After that the chief warriors will decide among themselves whose she is to be."

After that we said little, but continued along the wide trail in silence.

The ape-men numbered about two dozen, and I gathered that they were returning to their home, which they called Graypec. This was the tribe of Graypec. We had not been traveling very long before we came to a steep hill. It was an outcrop of sandstone. There were many round, dark holes in the face of the cliff, and ape-men and women moving about in front of them. Then these men were actually cave dwellers, I thought, remembering how I had first thought of them as cavemen. I felt I was learning fast.

The hill had alternate layers of sandstone that was fairly easy to burrow into, and stone that had had more clay in it when it was formed, and was consequently much harder. These harder ridges stood out like steps, and the caves were arranged in rows between them. Steps led up to the higher caves, and where it was very steep, ladders had been fashioned out of saplings and bound to shrubs growing out of the rock.

The company of cavemen poured into the open space in front of the caves, and, with grunts of satisfaction, sat down on the ground and fell to devouring the meat that hung roasting over many fires. My father doing likewise, I remembered my hunger and resolved to build up my strength before I did anything else. Accordingly, I picked up a piece of meat and began to gnaw. It was burned in one place and underdone in another, and parts of it were gritty where it had been dropped in the sand, but I was not disposed to be critical. I found it excellent.

A big fellow came up to me while I was eating and grunted, "Good work, youngster, capturing the yellow-hair; but you must be less foolhardy. The chief frowns on such rashness." Then, sharply, he added, "Where is your gun? You know the order: sleeping or waking you must always hold it in your hand, your mouth, or your feet."

"Don't be harsh with the boy," broke in my father, "he dropped it on the yellow ship when half conscious from the effect of the gas."

"What?" cried the big fellow. He seemed too astonished at the terrible nature of my offence to speak, as though he knew of no words to do justice to the matter. Finally he said: "This is too serious for me to deal with. The chief himself must see you. You will be lucky if he does not kill you."

As the big fellow lurched away on his short legs, my father went on servilely munching at the thigh-bone in his hands, then, when quite sure the other was out of hearing, he murmured to me:

"That fellow will get himself knifed in the back one day. Couldn't deal with you himself! Any other sub-chief would have given you the choice of losing your right to the woman or losing your status as hunter and warrior for half a year. And the chief made him sub-chief less than two moons ago! Ah, give a fool authority and he loses his head." So saying, he hid his face in the greasy meat again.

For a while we employed ourselves with filling our stomachs and lubricating our faces and hands. It was plain that I had an awkward hurdle to face if I had to interview this chief. My knees were shaky at the thought.

Conscience was worrying me, too. What I ought to be doing was looking for the prisoner and telling her that I was ready to help her; but so strange was everything here to me that it was probable that my help would be more harm than good to her, as it had been before.

"Now none of your foolhardiness when you see the chief," observed my companion, presently. "Curb your pride and temper, and take his insults meekly, otherwise your old father will lose his last son. I've been before him myself; he bellows and roars. Let him do all the talking and pretend to be afraid of him; that's the best way to manage him. Curse it, Grawtok has lost no time. Here comes the chief's personal servant."

Grawtok was the name of the sub-chief who had reported me. The messenger threaded his way carefully among the fires and the gorging cavemen who moved out of the way for him, and approached us. Curtly he announced that I was to follow him to the chief. "Now don't forget," rumbled my companion as I was led away.

CHAPTER FIVE

THE CHIEF'S RESIDENCE WAS ON THE GROUND FLOOR, AS IT were, a sort of verandah in front of the entrance, around which a crude effort had been made by means of carving and pigments to make the rock look like the head of a dragon. Into the mouth of this dragon we went. Inside, a guard sitting on his haunches rose and opened a massive iron gate.

I found myself in a large room around which I glanced curiously. Nothing that I had so far seen of the cavemen of Graypec had prepared me for what I saw here. I was expecting some rough place with a vulgar, showy splendor, but here were all the marks of a civilized being, one who knew the meaning of comfort and even luxury; at least, that was the impression it made on me, a stranger who had only the crude exterior of the place to base his judgment upon.

The floor was covered with a thick carpet of woven grass, soft and springy to the feet, and the walls were polished to a high degree of smoothness with fairly good pictures of flowers and animals hanging on them. There were a table and two chairs in what is called the rustic style, cleverly made, and a third chair was upholstered in blue cloth and looked quite inviting. But the feature of the room that was most startling of all was the one I noticed last; a globe of frosted glass was set in the ceiling and filling the room with soft light. What kind of man could this chief be? One does not expect the home of a caveman to be lit with neat electric lights.

I had been puzzled by the fact of these primitive creatures using such effective weapons as the one I was charged with losing, a dangerous combination of savagery and civilization; but here the problem became much more striking. Where, for one thing, could the current come from for the lights? Should I find modern dynamos and turbines here?

My guide indicated that I was to enter a small room opening off the large one, a room that was bare save for a hollow scooped in the floor and filled with water. After I had waited alone for several minutes, my guide entered again, but stopped short on seeing me.

"Get in and wash yourself, filthy creature," he snapped. "It would be an insult to the chief to enter his apartments in that filthy condition. Hurry, he is waiting!"

This still further convinced me that the chief was no ordinary caveman, but really I had been rather stupid in not guessing why I had been left in such an obvious bathroom. Without any regrets I stepped in. The water was tepid, contained soda, and there was a piece of strong soap and a brush, so that in a few minutes I got myself as clean, probably, as any caveman of Graypec ever was. There was a bar of solid gold set in the wall, but when I touched it, I got a sharp electric shock. I suppose it was put there to frighten the simple savages.

After shaking myself as a dog does, the only means of drying, I was ordered out and directed to follow my guide once more. He led me through two rooms and a passage, all lit just well enough for me to see that they were all furnished with strange fittings that I was full of curiosity to examine; but when I touched a chair in passing, to feel its texture, a sharp, "Hands off!" made me snatch my arm away.

Then we arrived in a room, which my guide indicated was the place where I would meet the chief.

It was a large room, dimly lighted, and with nothing but the absence of windows to suggest that it was underground. The ceiling was rounded, and I suppose the poor light was intended to give it an air of mystery. On the walls were life-like painting of fire-breathing animals, men with bat-like wings or with the heads of reptiles, and other designs intended to over-awe simple minds, like the sculptures of heathen temples. There were also dummies of nightmare creatures, dummies that startled one by suddenly moving or cackling hoarse laughter, as though at some secret joke. On the richly carved table were two vases from which poured vapor shot through with various colors. In the poor light it was eerie enough; but I looked for the wires carrying power to the mechanical figures, and found them. I listened for the scratch of the needles on the records producing their voices, and heard them. I looked for the wires carrying current to the colored lights hidden in the vases, and I saw them.

I was beginning to guess the answers to the questions that had been puzzling me; this chief of the cavemen of Graypec could be no savage ape-man himself; he must be a man of knowledge and intelligence who used his superior wisdom to keep these savages in subjection. That would explain their guns; he must have provided them. And if there was one civilized man on this world, there must be others, like the captive woman. But why, then, should this civilized chief allow his savage followers to attack one of his own kind—the "yellow hair," as they called her? It could be explained only by supposing that the chief was a traitor, a renegade, hostile to the rest of humanity— probably some outcast criminal seeking vengeance for imagined wrongs and using the ape-men as tools. As a matter of fact, this guess was wrong, but it was near enough for my purposes at the moment.

The room had been built in the shape of a round tunnel, always the best shape for an underground space, and the walls and floor had been added later. That meant that there must be spaces left behind the walls under the floor, where machinery, and perhaps men, might be hidden. On looking closely, I saw several concealed peepholes through which somebody might be watching me now.

Motioning me into a rough seat facing the table, my guide fiddled with the sides of the chair. Alarmed, I tried to break away, but I was too late; he had clamped a strong metal bar across my chest. Next he tried to fix my wrists, but I refused to allow it.

I heard a faint click as though some hidden person had closed a switch; and in sudden fear I tried to tear my body away from the chair. But it was impossible to escape from that brass bar, and that strange current began to work its will on me. It could not have been electricity as we know it; it had the curious effect of rendering me incapable of movement. I could not raise my arms or my legs; all I could move was my head. A peculiar numbness crept over me. The attendant padlocked my helpless arms to the chair and left me.

An ape-man in that position would probably have been in a state of pitiful terror. I was absolutely helpless; all I could now move were my eyes and mouth; even my neck had gone rigid. I could feel nothing of my limbs or trunk, neither warmth nor coldness nor the dampness of my bath, nor the hard seat under me. It was as though I were a head without a body, yet I was wide-awake. I was capable only of looking straight ahead, and of my body all I could see was just my knees and my toes. It was as though my body was dissolved in that swirling vapor, shot through and through with shifting colors; a savage would have thought that this was what had actually happened, and when, later, the current was turned off, he would imagine that, by an act of remarkable generosity, his body had been re-created for him out of its elements.

The door closed behind my guide, and I waited for the mysterious chief to show himself.

Now almost filling the room, the weaving smoke thinned as though swept aside by a strong draft. Then, where had been empty space a moment before, appeared the figure of a man.

He was a middle-aged man, fat and overfed, such a man as hundreds one meets in any modern city. He had fat cheeks, a broad nose and bulging eyes, and was dressed in a simple purple robe that hung from one shoulder and reached to his knees. He was glaring at me with concentrated ferocity and making passes through the air, for all the world like some fat uncle at some children's party, fondly imagining that he looks terrifying. For a moment I had a struggle not to laugh, but perhaps he thought I was only making a grimace of terror.

And the next moment I was in terror, yes, in actual fright. Because, you know, there was nothing there! I could see the nightmarish paintings on the walls and the mechanical dummies clearly *through* his body. He moved, and, in the conventional way of ghosts, passed right through a chair. Then he vanished into nothingness.

The smoke thickened, and something big moved away from in front of me. Then I knew how the conjuring trick had been worked, for it was nothing more. Everybody has looked into store windows and has seen objects in the street reflected in the glass, in the same way the man I had seen had been hidden from me while I had seen his reflection on a sheet of glass in front of me. The lights had been carefully arranged so that none of them shone on the glass, and in the duskiness one could not see the sheet at all. He himself stood in a very bright light, and when he turned the light out, his image vanished.

Under the cover of semi-darkness, the sheet of glass was moved away. Then the atmosphere cleared again, and the real man stood before me, his arms folded and a sardonic leer on his face.

"So you are promoted to the rank of warrior and hunter," he observed, slowly, "and the very first day that you carry the thunder-tube only a warrior may carry, you lose the sacred weapon you should guard with your life.

Do you realize the harm you may have done? Suppose, before rust makes it useless, it were to get into the hands of some intelligent animal! You would see your comrades falling one by one, shot from ambush."

In this the chief spoke the exact truth. To me it was the most astonishing thing of all in that strange world, Kilsona, that if, say, a lion or a wolf, were to pick up a fallen gun, he would examine it and would be quite likely to find out how to use it. Yet was it so strange? After all, we train animals to do things almost as clever, and the standards of intelligence in the wilds is always improving.

"You think," went on the chief, "that your madness has given you a right to this woman. You have lost that right and your status as warrior as well. The woman shall be mine."

He opened a door and called, and the captive girl, with her mop of yellow hair, walked slowly into the room. It was the first time I had really observed her closely, and I thrilled with admiration of her grace and courage. For, slight as she was, slender as a reed before the bulk of the flabby brute who grinned at her with greedy eyes, there was no fear in her bearing. Without posturing, she met his gaze with cold disdain. From him she turned to look at his weird pictures and dummies, and I saw his eyes flash with anger at her half-smile of contempt. Then she saw me and recoiled; and I was hurt, for I had forgotten that I was to her a repulsive savage.

Slim and straight she stood and looked the chief steadily in the eyes.

"Whatever your ambitions," she said, for she spoke in the tongue I understood and her voice was calm and distinct, "and whatever means you may use to further them, at least you are still a man. You would protect a helpless woman from these brutes."

He took her motionless face in his hands.

"Trust me," he said; "I will see that they do not harm you."

"You will return me to my people?"

He took a step towards her, but she stepped back so that his arms fell to his sides.

"Now, my pretty one," he urged, "do be reasonable. You know the cruel law of your people: death before capture. They saw your machine fall, know of your fight. Return to them and they, knowing that you had been alive in the hands of my warriors, would destroy you and wipe all mention of you from their records."

Her eyes fell in shame. "You have your servant here," she muttered, glancing at me, "to thank for my sin in being still alive."

"Yes, he has his uses," agreed the chief, "but he has also disgraced himself. Now by the law of my warriors, yes, I made it myself, anyone of them who is responsible for the capture of a woman of Teth-Shorgo has the first right to her."

She answered not, staring at him with contempt and fury.

"Your mate," he said, indicating me with a mocking smile. "You see," he went on, "why he was so brave, and now that I have seen you, I understand him. But so beautiful a lady need not be handed over to him if I say not; neither need you be returned to your own folk to be slain, so full of youth and vitality. Look at him and then at me, and choose between us!"

"Between the man who has sunk so low as to betray his kind," she said with bitter, icy distinctness, "and the subman who knows no better than to behave as an animal," her words now were shrill and fast, *"give me the caveman!"*

She had all a woman's natural cleverness in saying things that hurt, in striking where pride or vanity were greatest, but I was certain she did not mean what she said.

The effect on the man was all it was meant to be; her insulting reply dashed the confident leer from his face, leaving a sickly, dazed expression. Then came anger, the overbearing anger of a man who is not used to having his will thwarted. His face congested with fury, he struck at her. As she crashed to the floor and lay still, I was at first quite sure she was dead.

He kicked her unconscious body; then, catching my eye, he strode at me in such a rage that I thought he was going to kill me for witnessing his humiliation; but, when already menacing me with an iron club he had snatched from one of his mechanical figures, he checked himself. Dropping the weapon, he snarled:

"No, you can live, cub. To hand her over to you and the others is the best punishment for her. Let the tribe take her; I care not what happens." With that, he turned and vanished through a hidden door in the wall.

I found myself able to move again and staggered from the rough seat, only to fall awkwardly to the floor. For several minutes I was in agony as I fought to bring my body back to normal life.

I was relieved to find the girl still breathing, and seemingly suffering from nothing more than severe bruises. As I looked at her, one arm lifted above her head in futile attempt at defense, but she did not regain consciousness.

The attendant then entered, apparently with orders, for he gruffly told me to help him pick up the unconscious girl. Carrying her between us, like a feather in our powerful arms, we shuffled on our short legs through several rooms out into the light of the moon, for the sun had set.

CHAPTER SIX

MOST OF THE FIRES WERE OUT, BUT THOSE THAT REMAINED glowed redly. For the most part, the ape-men had retired to their caves, but many remained in the open around the fires, sleeping uneasily after overeating, or squatting on their haunches, or shuffling slowly about.

At the sight of us, there burst forth a series of guttural yells at which the sleepers all jumped to their feet, ready for danger; then seeing no cause for alarm, they allowed their eyes to become bleary with sleep again. But none of them lay down; all came crowding around us, poking with long fingers the flesh of the girl as she lay on the ground.

The attendant announced curtly that the prisoner was handed over to the tribe, then went back to his master's cave. The chief trained his servants well.

A dozen hands lifted the girl and carried her to the light of the fires, on which others were now throwing armfuls of small wood to produce a bright blaze.

"I claim this woman!" I cried, in a voice I tried to make as fierce as possible.

Few heeded me. I called again, louder: "I claim this woman by right of capture!"

There were bursts of laughter, derision, but I went on shouting until they listened to me.

"Be silent, cub," growled one. "You are no longer a warrior."

"You have lost your right," snapped another.

"The woman is mine by right," I bellowed, unable to argue but determined to stand my ground.

"You are behaving dangerously, infant," observed a huge, immensely powerful fellow, not unkindly.

Grawtok pushed himself forward, the sub-chief who had caused me to be taken before the chief.

"By the right of the sub-chiefs," he declared, "I am next on the list. She is mine."

"She is mine," I maintained, not without some sinking at the heart.

Without a sound he pivoted on his left arm, the knife from his ankle-sheath sweeping high in his right. Totally unprepared, for the distance had seemed to me much too far for such a blow, he might have struck me to the heart, had not a heavy, hurtling body knocked the arm aside. It was the man who claimed to be my father.

"Let the boy alone," he growled.

There was a gasping intake of breath from the on-lookers, who forgot the girl to crowd closely around us.

"By the order of the chief," cried Grawtok, trembling with fury, "it is death to strike a sub-chief, except in self defense."

"And that law," snarled back my defender, "allows of one exception only, the case of a father defending his son! Such is the wise law of the chief, to prevent the weakening of the tribe by the slaughter of the defenseless young by bullies. You, Grawtok, are a bully; the tribe is weary of your overbearing ways. I challenge you to combat!"

Gone now was servility, rage taking its place. He had courage, that supposed father of mine, for Grawtok had at least a fifty-pound advantage in weight besides a much longer reach.

"By the law," growled Grawtok, "I need not fight; I may report you for punishment for defying my authority. I appeal to the other sub-chiefs present."

He called them by name, and they came forward, three massive cavemen. It was plain that Grawtok was not popular with them. For a few moments they conferred, then the biggest of all, the phlegmatic fellow who had warned me I was behaving dangerously, voiced the opinion of them all.

"It is true Grawtok need not fight if he does not wish to, but we consider he has now his personal status to think of. He has been called a bully, and we remember occasions when he has been accused of cowardice. To our knowledge, he has never given proof of the falsity of these charges; we consider that, in this case, if he wishes to keep the respect of the tribe, he would be wise to win it by the force of his arms."

Grawtok's eyes opened wide with astonishment, and I heard gasps of surprise from those around. Afterwards I learned that this was the first occasion when the select body of sub-chiefs had failed to support one of their number against one of the rank and file.

"I will fight," snarled Grawtok with a look that made me tremble for the courageous man who had come between me and danger. "We will fight with our knives." He held, point foremost, the foot-long edged weapon from his ankle-sheath.

"One knife each, only," said the spokesman.

The combatants circled each other warily, taking deep breaths to insure a good supply of oxygen for the effort that was to come; each kept his eyes fixed on those of the other, and the palm of a free hand on the ground, for the slightest wavering of either, the least relaxation of alertness, would be a sign for the other to whirl upon him.

For a full minute it was a conflict of wills, a slow creeping around, each waiting for the other to drop his eyes or make a false step; then, so quickly that I could not follow his movements, Grawtok sprang. For an instant or so in the swirl of green arms and bodies, I could not see what was happening; then I was aware that the other had avoided him and was himself springing.

Grawtok's arm deflected the blow aimed at his throat, a red gash appearing on his forearm; then the two bodies were locked together. Each held the other's knife-arm by the wrist and sought to loosen the grip on his own arm. Back and forth they struggled, neither gaining the advantage, until my father suddenly jumped, seizing the other around the middle with both his legs. Backwards he went and they rolled on the ground, Grawtok on top, but it was obvious that, for all his greater weight, the pressure on his stomach was causing him considerable distress.

There was a short knife in Grawtok's left foot, and with it he stabbed at my father's side. It was an action hidden from most of the onlookers, and I saw the distress on his opponent's face.

I jumped forward, shouting: "Grawtok fights unfairly. He has two knives!"

Seizing the limb that held the weapon, I dragged it back into the light of the blazing brushwood, that all might see. Hands gripped me, and there were confused shouts of, "Stand back, cub!" while others said, "There is truth in what he says!"

Strong arms dragged Grawtok off his victim, my father making game efforts to rise and continue the battle but collapsing. The spokesman of the sub-chiefs thrust the second knife under Grawtok's nose, demanding, "What is this?"

"He produced it and struck at me," declared Grawtok, "and I took it from him."

"He lies," I cried; "I saw him take it from an ankle-sheath!"

The spokesman folded his arms and looked grim.

"Cub, all this trouble is of your making. Now you accuse one of us of a crime for which death by torture is the only just punishment. You must fight, you and he whom you have accused, and may the God of the Lightning, whose priest is our chief, give victory to he who speaks truth. But, by the law, when a warrior fights one who is not yet a warrior, and not instructed in the use of weapons, they must fight with bare hands only."

I could not have been suited better, for, though Grawtok was twice my weight, I flattered myself that my skill in boxing would hold him off.

Both of us had our sheaths taken away to prevent further fouls, then Grawtok hurled himself on me. I stood in what must have seemed to them a curious attitude, upright, left arm and shoulder foremost, trying to adapt my boxing experience to these unaccustomed limbs. As he came on, I measured the distance and struck out with my left, putting all my strength into one terrific blow.

Probably they had never seen a straight left before. Full in the face he caught it, all the weight of his ponderous hurtling body adding force to the blow. It was like hitting a brick wall, an impact calculated to fell an ox. The violence of it nearly broke my wrist, shook me to the heels.

Yet he came on. Incredibly, impossibly, he came on, and gripped me around the waist. Had he not been half-unconscious from the blow, I might have died in the first few seconds under his hands, while I stood motionless from astonishment. Then the fighting spirit of the caveman came uppermost; the pain of his grip brought me to myself, set me tearing with my smaller arms at his back, all thought of method of fighting banished in red rage that sought only to wound and tear, to destroy before I myself be destroyed. Our bodies were soon slippery and clotted with blood.

I found myself on the ground, underneath, Grawtok seeking to reach my throat and tear the arteries. I forgot to claw, and struggled only to defend my throat, while he concentrated on reaching the vital spot. Slowly, inevitably, his enormously superior weight was winning; soon one of his paws was at my throat, but still I was able to prevent his using it for a while.

Until now it had been the green ape-man that struggled for life, but now, with death near at hand, I had a moment of calmness and remembered my other life. All the resources of my two personalities were combined in that last effort, before all was blotted out.

His other arm, the one at my side, was bent at the wrist, palm towards forearm. I remembered a ju-jitsu trick whereby the hand is bent, palm towards forearm; it was a simple-looking hold I had been shown long ago, but yet it is one of the most painful in ju-jitsu.

With a sudden twist I seized that arm. He, concentrating on the other, heeded not but took the opportunity to secure a grip on my throat. As I put on pressure, his grip relaxed; he howled with pain. As a rule, these men fought to death without a sound; but I showed no mercy, for my life was in the balance; I pressed until the joint snapped and Grawtok's body went limp.

Dizzily I got to my feet, Grawtok lying as one dead. There was no movement from those around, the cavemen waiting either for Grawtok to rise and continue the battle or for me to slay the helpless brute.

"Good work, boy," said my father.

It surprised me to see him, for I had thought his wounds fatal; yet he stood there grinning broadly and, though plastered with blood, seemingly almost as well as ever. As a matter of fact, his injuries had been lighter than I had supposed, and the power of recovery possessed by these men was astonishing.

Then I looked at Grawtok and gasped. For the first time I saw the effect of my punch; his nose was smashed and the front part of his face partly pushed in, blue swellings making the rest of it almost unrecognizable. Yet he had fought on! I felt a new respect for the vanquished brute.

"Are you satisfied?" asked the spokesman. "It is at your option to slay him or to take your chance of his vengeance when he recovers."

"Let him live," I replied. Grawtok was now a pitiful object, sitting up and moaning feebly. The spokesman bent over the fallen sub-chief.

"Either," he declared, "the cub is a tremendous warrior, or the God of Lightning did indeed give him strength. He strikes, and his foe looks as though a rock had fallen on him. He grips, and behold!"

He shook the injured arm, showing how the broken joint allowed the paw to flap helplessly about, heedless of the fact that Grawtok screamed and fainted again as he did so.

"Cub," he said, "you are not a warrior, yet I proclaim you the greatest fighter in the tribe!"

I would rather have been without this distinction, for, in the event of my being challenged for the "title," I was by no means confident of being able to get another such hold, my knowledge of ju-jitsu being of the slightest; but I could not help smiling at the delighted way my foster father preened himself on hearing these words.

Then I remembered there was something still to be attended to. Ah! the girl. I asked after her.

"She is yours as long as you want her. The women are taking her to your cave."

I was some seconds grasping the full meaning of this; then I saw that my object was won. Quickly I looked around and saw a ribald group of women dragging the captive roughly towards the cliff.

"Handle her gently!" I directed them, sharply. They stopped and stared at me, huge females nearly all of them bigger than I.

"Carry her yourself, whelp!" snapped one, giving the captive a blow that knocked her spinning, to fall at my feet. I wished now I had not interfered, for I had no idea which cave was my own.

Though I whispered to the girl that I was her friend who would protect her in every way, still she refused to heed, and, as I bent to pick her up, she turned on me and, all restraint gone in her despair, sank sharp, white teeth into my arm. A cackle of laughter sounded from the women. Again I spoke soothingly and tried to pick her up, but again she beat me off.

I felt that I was making a fool of myself, but again my father came to help me; he picked the girl up by the legs, and I carried her by the arms, so that we managed her between us easily.

"Where are you going?" he asked sharply. We were before a cunningly hidden hole in the rock that I had not noticed. Passing inside we found ourselves in a small, rough imitation of the chief's burrow, with heaps of herbage as the only furnishings and lighted by dim lamps in the ceiling that never went out, but which left most of the place in gloom.

My companion closed a heavy bronze gate across the entrance, bolted it with bolts that could not be reached from outside, and we shuffled in together. Breaking from us, the captive crouched, trembling, in a dark corner.

We were in a roomy cave, set well back in the rock, yet there must have been some outlet for the air, for it was quite fresh.

A thickset female shambled forward, her eyes fixed in a hostile stare on the prisoner, and spoke gruffly to my father, who indicated me. I assumed this to be my mother, but as a matter of fact it was about her tenth successor; for marriages among the men of Graypec were on the same plan as the matings of wild creatures, usually lasting for one year only, from spring to autumn. They soon tired of each other, and when there was a child it would be brought up by the father to be a warrior if it were a male, but if it happened to be a mere female, little interest was taken in it.

The present mate of my father, on learning that the strange woman was mine and not a rival for herself, took no further notice of her, nor of me. The two settled themselves at one end of the cave and went to sleep.

Gathering myself a heap of herbage and pushing another towards the captive, I tried to make myself comfortable. I felt absurdly embarrassed, for I had no idea what to say to her.

We sat in silence, I perplexed and divided against myself, she tense like an animal about to spring.

"Several times," I said at last, "I have assured you I mean no harm to you, why do you not believe me?"

"But you are a caveman," she murmured at last.

"I seem to be a savage, but I am not," I said. I fumbled for words. "This is not my body. I don't know how to tell you—"

"Transferred personality?" she gasped. "Is it possible? It is said that in the days of man's greatness, thousands of years ago, before humanity split into separate streams, when one man could speak and the whole world hear, when the world was so ruled that only in a few places was it necessary to carry arms, long, long before the coming of the Larbies, that learned men could transfer the personality of one man to the brain of another; but it was never perfect. It resulted in the two personalities warring in each of the two brains, and any attempt to reverse the process often resulted in confusion. Is it possible these wonders of the forgotten past can be repeated in this weary world today?"

My problem of explaining myself was already partly solved, yet I lay still with nothing to say. What could I say? I was like a newborn child.

"Then your fight," she said at last, "was not to win me, but to protect me?"

"You saw?"

"The women held me, made me look, told me you were fighting for possession of me." She shuddered. "I hoped you would win, you looked so small against that monster, but when you came to pick me up, I found you were so big and terrifying that it seemed you could not be the same man. What town do you come from?"

I tried to say, "From another world," but the nearest I could get at it in that language was, "From another place," waving my hand vaguely upwards.

"What town?" There was tense suspicion now in her voice.

"Another town, far away, up. A very long way up, among the stars."

"A planet? But all the other inhabited planets were abandoned ages ago. Who would stay on them when life was so much easier here? The secret of inter-planetary flight has been lost for thousands of years." She jumped to her feet, eyeing me with loathing. "You lie! I believe you are a transferred personality, but you are from no other world. You are from Gorlem, the only place where men could possibly know how to do such things. You are a spy! I will denounce you to your tribe."

"And would they heed your cries? Remember the circumstances under which we are thrown together here."

Like a pricked balloon, she collapsed. "It is true. To unmask one of the common enemy, but to be helpless because of this absurd internal strife! Yet," her voice rose to normal, "you do not kill me, or even harm me. I do not understand. Ah, I know; you are torturing me, keeping me in fear and doubt!" Hopelessly she stared across the cave.

I was near to losing my temper, for I had been through much that day. "It seems you are determined not to believe me," I declared. "I know nothing of your Gorlem, but am weary of talking at cross-purposes. Leave me to sleep."

Curled up like a cat, it was long before I slept, for the events of the day and the problems they raised kept milling around in my brain, growing ever more puzzling as my brain became duller with sleep and my headache fiercer.

Twisting and turning and several times rising to rearrange my grassy couch, every time I had looked I saw the captive woman sitting in the half-light, motionless, her eyes fixed on me. At last I slept, for I dreamed that I was tied down and that she bent over me, murder in her glance.

There was a sub-stratum of truth in my dream, for I felt the lightest possible touch on my ankle. Instantly the automatic response of the caveman jerked me wide awake, made me jump to my feet, ready for combat, one hand holding the hand that had been stealthily drawing the dagger from its sheath. One advantage of short legs was that one could get up very quickly.

Facing me, her eyes running with tears at the pain of my unconsciously strong grip, was the prisoner.

"So you would murder me in my sleep," I reproached her.

She was silent.

"Why will you not believe me when I say I mean you no harm? How can I convince you?"

Her face downcast, she shot me a glance of misery. "To me, personally, you are good; but you are a man of Gorlem, a sworn foe of both branches of humanity. As a man, I respect you, but as a member of that community, I hate you; for you seek the destruction of my kinsman, and of all the rest of mankind. Under the orders and directions of the Larbies, we must fight."

Picking up the fallen blade I handed it to her, hilt foremost.

"Take it," I said. "If I closed my eyes so that you could strike me to the death if you wished, would that convince you that I am not your enemy?"

Unwillingly, she took the keen steel blade she had taken such pains in her efforts to obtain secretly. It seemed to fascinate her.

"Come close; hold it to my throat," I invited, but she held off.

Closing my eyes, I laid down; but, as was only natural, I watched through narrowed lids.

Like one in a trance she came towards me, blade foremost. With agonizing slowness and hesitation, she advanced until I felt the point resting against the flesh.

Five, ten seconds I waited, frozen, not breathing, every muscle taut. Then I knew she would not strike; she had hesitated too long.

"You are a spy, but I am a traitor," she moaned, dropping her arms. "I cannot do it."

Her nearness was an intoxicating thing, flowing through my veins like fire, overwhelming all reason, all self-restraint. I threw my arms around her. If ever I was near to death it was then! Her eyes flashed and the deadly blade shot up to my throat. But again she did not strike and the pressure of the steel eased up.

"Release me, please," she pleaded. "Remember, although you have the mind of a civilized man, you have the body of a savage, and your embrace is not pleasant."

I let go of her and again I tried to sleep, but got up to ask for the return of the knife.

Refusing at first, when she saw that I was prepared to wrest it from her by force, she tossed it so that it fell on the dried grass beside me. From then on I slept soundly with my hand on the hilt.

CHAPTER SEVEN

A HAND ON MY SHOULDER ROUSED ME. IT WAS MY FATHER. His mate was absent but the captive slept, one arm above her head like a child.

"We go hunting soon." He glanced at the girl. "Be patient and treat her not too roughly at first, and she will perhaps make you a good mate. Son, women are difficult creatures to handle; learning to hunt is child's play compared to learning to manage a mate. Take too little notice of them and they become sulky and bad-tempered; pet them overmuch and they grow spoiled, which is far worse. One's first half-dozen matings are seldom very successful, unless one is wise enough to choose only experienced matrons, as few young men are. I remember my first mate; I was her first man, and we quarreled and fought so that the sub-chiefs parted us after a month, and we both had empty caves for the rest of the year. Taught us both a lesson. Four years afterwards we mated again and we got on very well. You see, experience made all the difference. Nobody is a really good husband or wife until the fourth time.

"My second mate—"

While he rambled on in this fashion about the peculiar relations of the sexes in Graypec, we left the cave and emerged into the bright day. A sub-chief handed me a weapon similar to the one I had lost.

"Then Grawtok is dead?" asked my father.

"Less than two hours after the fight. His conqueror takes his weapon," said the sub-chief, turning away.

Though I had seen the broken bone of Grawtok's cheek exposed to the air, and knew that disease must strike at such a compound fracture, I was amazed that it should do so with such rapidity.

I would have preferred to have spent the day poking about the cave village—the question of where the electric power came from interesting me particularly—but I was clearly expected to join in this hunt, and so had to be content with exploring the surrounding country instead.

A group of warriors were ready, and we started off across the plain. There was no stopping for food, for the custom was to eat but one meal a day, and that in the evening. Among the trees, we went more carefully, sending out scouts in parties of three, or climbing trees for a sight of game. Although we covered many miles, we never got really far from the village of Graypec, for the boundaries of our hunting grounds, unmarked but exactly known, were between three and five miles away in four directions. To the north, south, and east were the territories of other tribes, and to the west a belt of barren country lay between us and the sea.

Once I wandered off a little way on my own, and the result was a torrent of abuse from my father. I gathered that it was always dangerous to be alone in the game country, owing to the alertness and intelligence of the wild creatures. Seeing a man alone, they would hurl heavy stones from behind bushes, or big animals would dash out one's brains from behind, or the coils of a huge snake would drop around one's neck and jerk one up into a tree. Very seldom was the victim allowed a chance to cry out; the only safety lay in numbers, for all animals had a wholesome respect for our guns, and knew that a dead man's comrades would exact vengeance.

When it came to the turn of my father to join a scouting party, I went with him as a spectator, and we pushed cautiously through the breast-high undergrowth. Our movements were cat-like in their stealthiness and silence.

"Where is Teth-Shorgo?" I whispered to my father, remembering the chief's use of the word as the name of the place the captive woman, Issa, had come from.

"A town four hours' journey to the south. I've been there—great cliffs built by men out of rocks you can see through, with people living in them. They say it was a splendid place once, but most of it's in ruins now. Even now, it is said, there are places in it more wonderful than our chief's home; but for my part, I'd much sooner live in a nice, dry cave hollowed out of natural rock than in the most wonderful-looking house with wire-netting in the windows and the roof fallen in. Wild beasts roam the streets on dark nights when the weather is not too hot."

"And when it is very hot?"

"The smells are too bad, even for the animals."

I was shocked. His words ruined my half-formed plans, for I had dreamed of returning Issa to her own people in the end, somehow overcoming the difficulty of the punishment that awaited her there, and even of myself becoming an inhabitant of Teth-Shorgo.

"Won't they send a rescue party to find our captive?" I asked, bringing out an idea that had been in my mind for some time.

"Why should they? They don't care what happens to each other. They are too anxious for the safety of their own skins."

So that was it. I had wondered why the men of the town did not make war on and destroy these hairy brutes of the forests, but it seemed that the real problem was why the cavemen did not destroy the men of the town.

"The warriors," went on my companion, "would be glad enough to see the foul place wiped off the land, but the chiefs forbid it. The numbers of anyone tribe are too few for the purpose, and the tribes will not combine. Besides, even the men of Teth-Shorgo have some uses; they make guns and visit Graypec ten times a year to tend the machines that feed our lights. Under the waterfalls they go and get all greasy messing about with the great wheels that roar as they spin. In return we leave their town in peace, and give them meat and fruits to carry back."

Getting bolder, I asked who the men of Gorlem were.

Startled at the word, he looked anxiously around, then muttered in agitated tones:

"My boy, you're asking a lot of questions today. It would be much better for you to leave such problems to older heads. Confine your attention to hunting, for the present. It is unsafe to be too inquisitive.

"Nobody knows who the men of Gorlem are, at least nobody at Graypec except the chief. All that we others know is that we are at war with them, for they are trying to conquer the land and destroy all other men. Every cave village and all towns like Teth-Shorgo yield an annual quota of warriors for the war; they are taken away and never heard of again. Be careful, or you may be one of those to go from Graypec this year. They are never heard of again, and they fight under the direction of the all-wise, all-powerful Larbies."

The last words were almost chanted, the final phrase being uttered in hushed tones of awe. He stood quite motionless, his eyes fixed and without expression.

"And now, silence!" he barked at me more sharply than ever before, and from then on we thought of nothing but the hunting.

A scouting party presently reported that a herd of about two dozen "ollideps" had been sighted, and the news revived our drooping spirits, for nothing substantial had come the way of this group of hunters for three days, and the group was faced with the prospect of short rations if its luck did not change. The older hunters held a conference.

The ollideps were grazing in a wide clearing with woods on three sides of them, the fourth side being a passage forming a natural bottleneck. There was no hope of approaching the herd closely, the question therefore being which way they would run when disturbed. On becoming aware of men, they might slip away through the trees and there would then be the tedious job of tracking them, probably ending in their escape into the hunting grounds of another tribe. If, however, they could be induced to bolt in a panic, they would keep to the open and rush along the bottleneck, where men might lie in wait among the trees.

Accordingly we split into parties, the main company making a wide detour to reach the far side of the clearing while six men, myself with them, went to the passage along which the game were to be driven.

To my surprise, my companions began to cut sticks in the woods, selecting a certain parasitic growth that ran to great lengths, the stem of which was as pliable as a rope. Trimming off the branches with their daggers, they produced quite serviceable lariats, to one end of which they tied a stone. These, and not their guns, were to be used in bringing down the quarry.

Ordering me to keep out of sight, they selected hiding places that left them room to whirl their weighted stems, then for a long while all was still. At last, looking out, I saw strange-looking animals bounding towards us.

In writing of the fauna of Kilsona, I have used the words tigers, lizards, and wolves, but my readers should understand that I mean creatures something like these earthly animals. A naturalist might say that what I call tigers more nearly resembled leopards, or that my wolves were more akin to big coyotes; but there are no earthly beasts in any way resembling these round, jumping olli-deps, except, in some respects, kangaroos. Their bodies like round rubber balls, their little heads set on long, straight necks, they bounded along, their two legs bending under them like springs each time they landed. Perhaps a little smaller than prize Percheron horses, they could leap twenty feet into the air and had the speed, it seemed to me, of racing autos. The pounding of their feet was like the booming of big drums.

A lariat hissed through the air, wrapping itself around the legs of the leader, who fell with a crash; seemingly unable to check their headlong flight, seven or eight more followed on, and as my companions sent their coiled, weighted stems whizzing through the air, each one brought down one of the heavy beasts. One of the ollideps broke through and fled madly, filling the air with shrill screams.

The screaming and bellowing was now deafening, the terrified herd scattering in all directions across the plain, but those who had fallen lay still, their necks broken. Following on, the beaters killed two more with their guns, but the rest escaped. Our bag amounted to ten, at which all seemed well satisfied.

It puzzled me how the heavy bodies were to be conveyed to Graypec, but the carcasses were skinned on the spot, the waste matter and most of the bones removed, and they were tied with thongs into rough bundles. Two men carried each body and we returned, bloody but happy, to Graypec.

CHAPTER EIGHT

THESE METHODS, ADOPTED WHENEVER PRACTICAL, WERE NOT always used, as it was not at all times easy to send the game stampeding past an ambush in such a way as to enable the killers to use the lariats. Then the explosive bullets had to be resorted to, but not only was this regarded as waste of valuable ammunition, but also animals killed in this way were not considered such good eating as those with their necks broken in a fall caused by a lariat.

Hunting was always difficult, owing to the intelligence and alertness of our victims; they possessed a power of putting two and two together that was almost uncanny. Man is the only thinking animal, but here on Kilsona were many animals that could think a little. Man's rule tottered.

About another thousand years, I reckoned, would see mankind on Kilsona extinct; perhaps it would be better so, now that his proud position was lost and a few machines, implements, and crumbling houses were all that remained of his one-time glory.

I found myself wondering why he had fallen. Had it been mere laziness, due to science making life too easy? Issa spoke of two branches of mankind, the cavemen being one branch and her own people of the city of Teth-Shorgo belonging to the other. She had also spoken of the Larbies, whom she, and all the others, seemed to dread.

Who were the "men of Gorlem?"

Why should the chief of the ape-men be a comparatively well-formed man?

These were the questions that puzzled me for many days, and to which I got no answers. Issa became terrified when I questioned her, and my father curtly told me to hold my tongue if I valued my safety. It was plain that our numbers were dwindling, for though food was fairly plentiful, fatal accidents were many. We had many empty caves.

The girl whose name was pronounced "Ice-ah," became, to all outward appearances, resigned to being my mate. We kept up that fiction, though, in fact, we kept apart, and she mixed with the others on terms of tolerated inferiority. Yet, privately, she still regarded me as an enemy, as though we shared some guilty secret.

Men from Teth-Shorgo, weak, poor specimens of men as I had expected, came to inspect our simple power plant and took away ollidep meat and fruits in their airplane. While they were about, Issa hid herself.

Between the two races, I preferred the men of the caves. Rough and primitive as they were, they were clever in their own way and had their codes of honor and hated cowards and bullies. Ordinary humanity, forced to live as they lived, would have been much as they were. Their world was so hard, food was so difficult to obtain, and they were so surrounded with danger that their whole lifetime was fully occupied with necessities. They lived for the present, with little thought of the past and less for a future that, unless one kept one's eyes and ears wide open, would not concern one.

They had amazing strength and endurance and great courage. I have told how Grawtok fought on when fatally injured, and father-love was so strong that I saw several fathers plunge into danger to defend their sons, once with fatal results. Hunting packs often did thirty miles of rough going a day, and hunters would lie motionless for hours in prickly thickets, their green skin and hair making them almost invisible.

Their little pistols—I never found out how they worked—had handles, a sort of bulb with switches, and a firing button. They would produce explosive missiles, the stupefying blue gas, or a death ray. The latter, however, was seldom used, since it rendered meat poisonous. Instantly fatal if hitting a vital spot at twenty yards, it took longer to operate at a distance, though there was no theoretical limit to its range. By peering through what looked like a fragment of green glass at the side of the weapon, one saw a spot of light playing on what one was aiming at—light invisible to anyone not using a similar crystal. Much as I longed to look inside these guns, I was told that any attempt to do so would result in a violent explosion, and I never had the courage to test it.

Gradually I became used to being a caveman, nearly forgetting my past. Somehow, I felt my brother could never locate me or distinguish me from the other green men. I have explained how I had taken Issa into my cave for her own safety, and that I had resolved, while keeping up an appearance of being mated to her, that we should actually remain apart; but in this I reckoned without Issa herself. She had never known in her hard life the kindness with which I treated her, and she became more and more affectionate towards me, while I, for my part, was fighting a losing battle, for I loved her. In her simple way she could see nothing to come between us—didn't I like her, she demanded, weeping bitterly. One may keep a resolution for weeks; then comes a moment of weakness, and all one's efforts are wasted. Mary Winifred, wife of Learoy Spofforth, seemed a vague, distant figure, and the doings of Kastrove, the caveman, to concern her less and less. In the end, Issa and I became mates.

She still regarded me as a "man of Gorlem," as though we shared some guilty secret she tried to forget.

My curiosity about that mysterious term grew, and I found, after two distressing scenes with her, that she would do nothing to define the term to me. I began to make practice of asking others who these men were, and who the Larbies were, inquiries that produced only embarrassment or rage, according to the individual questioned. I could learn nothing.

Aware as I was of attracting unfavorable attention, I persisted until my father gruffly warned me that the sub-chiefs, and, it was said, the chief himself, had begun to notice my ways, and that I must desist if I wished to live.

One day, while out hunting, the massive, taciturn spokesman of the sub-chiefs who had taken charge of events during my fight with Grawtok and since then had ignored me, suddenly said: "Kastrove, come with me!"

Astonished, for I had thought him unaware of my existence, I did so. It was a windy day, promising storms, and one could see for long distances. Never speaking, we went together up a steep hillside, up and up, climbing gentle slopes, sheer precipices and boulder-strewn gorges, until we came out into the open and could feel the bracing, salt-laden wind from the sea on our bodies. On we went, over undulating, chalky downs, until the land ended as though cut off at our feet, and far below, at the foot of overhanging cliffs, was the white foam of an angry sea. Below us were little white birds, and above a steel-gray flying ship, shaped rather like the one Issa had been flying before the breakdown that led to her capture, only much larger, sailed quickly and silently by. There were none of the semi-transparent yellow ships that came from or went to the city of Teth-Shorgo, for the weather was too rough for them to venture aloft.

"Cub," said my companion as we lay on our bellies looking out to sea, "raise your gun, press the trigger—no, no, put the lever at 'safety' first, thus—and look towards the horizon through the green crystal. Now tell me, what do you see?"

I saw nothing worth speaking about, and said so.

"Look carefully. Search!"

Then I saw it, a conical island, far out to sea, from which shone two penciled searchlights, wavering and flickering about the sky. To the naked eye there was nothing.

"There they are, cub, the Larbies you are so interested in. Two hours swim from the shore—if you escaped the fishes."

His voice was tense and low, but whether as a warning or reproof, or whether the distant object caused his excitement, I know not.

We lay still. A storm cloud passed over and wetted us; the sun dipped towards the horizon, but we moved not. I thought of the warriors, anxious to return to the caves and impatient for our reappearance; but I had learned my etiquette too well to make the first move.

"Cub, there is something strange about you, something I do not understand. I knew it when you dashed past me in that mad rush to capture the yellow-haired woman, and I was sure of it when you conquered Grawtok by means of some art I do not know; for that was not done by sheer strength, neither were you aided by the God of the Lightning, as I declared to the tribe.

"I am old, and these eyes have seen many things that others have no suspicion of. When I see a sign of the science-magic of the ancient days, it is as plain to me as a spark of fire in the dark; and while others wonder, I partly understand."

His huge hands rested on my wrists, gentle, yet holding me as helpless as a newborn babe in his colossal grasp.

"Cub, I am old and near my end. To one so young as you, life seems endless; only one near the end knows how very short it really is. I have lived longer than any other in the memory of the tribe, and I have kept my strength. I could, thanks to my experience, beat any warrior of Graypec now, but in a little while I shall begin to crack up. Then—well, there are others jealous of my position, and the chief himself would not be sorry to be rid of one who knows so much. Yes, I know the mutterings of the tribe, in the same way they muttered against my predecessor, forty years ago. I seem to speak of the chief disrespect-fully, but I am too old to fear even him; he is but a young-ster, the offspring of a cave father and a yellow-haired woman who had been captured by him, even such as your Issa.

"But before I die, I would do something for the benefit of the tribe—not by the directions of yonder creatures," he waved his arm out to sea, "nor of the ambitions of the chief, but of the wisdom of one who has seen much and has no longer any personal desires to gratify."

He had risen and was standing over me, still holding me to the ground. With one foot he took my gun out of my hand, then, holding my wrists, lifted me to my feet, then off the ground, for he was much taller than I was. Holding me at arms' length, he advanced so that he stood at the very edge and I dangled over the sea. All this while discipline forbade me to struggle; indeed, a sudden movement on my part might have overcome his uncertain balance and sent us both pitching over the edge.

Imagine the enormous strength that could thus hold, suspended at the length of his arms, what was in effect a heavy, full-grown man, and yet not to tremble but to stand as firm as a rock! Two thousand feet below the waves beat on shingles and boulders.

My heart pounded and sweat broke from every pore. I set my teeth in a terrible effort to control my fear, to retain mastery of my mind.

He began to swing me right and left like a pendulum, then suddenly let me drop. Such a wave of terror swept over me that I lost all control of my mind, surrendered to a paroxysm of fear...

Then my back struck the rock and my fall was arrested; for he had not let go of me.

I lay on my back on the grassy downs, but my brain was unable to understand the messages of my senses. It seemed that the earth and sky spun around and around, first one beneath me and then the other—that I was falling headlong and rocks and waves were leaping up at me.

"Fear no longer," I heard his voice presently; "you are safe now, though for a moment I almost decided to let you drop. When you have quite recovered, I will explain why I did that."

For a time I listened to the pounding of my heart, then at last I was able to rest a steady gaze on him and to listen once more with attention.

CHAPTER NINE

"KNOW, MAN," SAID THE SPOKESMAN OF THE SUB-CHIEFS, "for you are no caveman cub, that I can read the thoughts of others—sometimes. Ordinarily one's mind sets up natural barriers of resistance to the thought-reader, but at times, by the will of a practiced subject, or during great weakness or great fear, those barriers are lowered and an expert may read. I knew you were no man of Graypec, and that only by what we call science-magic did you get here. Knowing that, the chief or any of the tribe, or even of the people of Teth-Shorgo, would have destroyed you at once, for we have forgotten our science while the Larbies have much, and the men of Gorlem some, knowledge. Our ancestors knew more than either.

"I noticed your endless questions, the very facts that have caused the chief to suspect you, that have put you in danger now, and they caused me to think that you were not from Gorlem, neither were you a spy of the Larbies. I set myself to find out. It was useless asking questions; I could do it only by reading your thoughts. So I held you suspended over the sea until the natural resistance of your mind broke down.

"Much of what was in your brain I did not understand. I still did not know where you came from, and in disgust I nearly dropped you; but I persisted and gleaned the knowledge that at least you are not hostile to us; you simply know nothing about anything. Your ignorance is surprising, but your mind is free; I noted that particularly your mind is free.

"Here on this cliff-top there is no living creature within earshot. Not even a bird whose uncomprehending brain might record the sounds of my voice, can catch my low tones. As far as it is ever possible to be certain of no hostile being catching my words in some strange apparatus, it is possible here. Otherwise I would not risk your life in talking to you as I am about to do. My own life matters not."

For a while he was silent, thoughtfully gazing to the west, where the sky was beginning to glow red with the approaching sunset. Then he continued.

"Know, man, that there is no God of the Lightning. That worship was invented by my ancestors, in whom some remnant of ancient wisdom still lingered, as a symbol of the power of the lightning, the power men once controlled and whereby they ruled Kilsona—yes, and whereby our fathers still hoped men might again be masters of this planet. Alas for their hopes, now that this religion of the Larbies has taken the place of the religion they invented!

"You knew the physical tyranny of Grawtok, whom you slew, but there is a greater, far harsher tyranny, the tyranny of the mind—yes, the tyranny of yonder creatures, to whom mankind has been sold!" He stretched out a massive arm and pointed at the distant island, whose wavering pencils of light could still be seen through the green crystals.

"Nearly all we cavemen and the people of Teth-Shorgo—sad remnant of a mighty race—are under that tyranny, whose worst feature is that the victim is always unaware of his servitude. Some of us, the very oldest, know it, but every year our numbers grow fewer. All the young are subject; we cannot find one to whom to pass on our message. But you—your mind is free—though why, I know not."

Having spoken, he stopped, as if stricken silent. Finally he rose and, as though I were not there, set off down the slope. Never again did he show that he knew of my existence.

Brave, lonely, independent mind in a colony of brutes! The end he had foreshadowed for himself came about a week later; and forthwith craven beings who once cowered at his approach talked of the dead lion with contempt, and would have thrown his body out in the open to be dealt with by the natural scavengers of the plain, had not the other sub-chiefs, anxious for the dignity of their rank, intervened. His body was burned on a pyre after an elaborate ceremony that included a torchlight procession, much howling and dancing and beating of drums. The chief himself put on a fearsome headdress and looked on at the end of his servant; the chosen successor lighted the fire. There had been a similar funeral for Grawtok, but under the circumstances I had not been allowed to witness it.

What the dead man had told me, illuminating so far as it went, was still too vague and general to help me much; but I have given it in detail as it was the only definite guidance I got for many months as to the state of the world. It gave me many clues to work on. I understood why the Larbies were spoken of with bated breath, as a religious fanatic might speak of heaven. I also understood the strange way in which Issa regarded me; it was a thing planted in her mind by some outside influence, and persisted *against her will.* I was an enemy and she was powerless to throw off the idea.

That the warnings of my father and of the dead leader as to the danger my persistent curiosity had led me into were justified was proved in a dramatic fashion soon after the latter died. I had arrived home after a fruitless hunt, tired but apparently well, when my left side began to irritate me. This I took little notice of at first, but slowly the pain increased until I was in agony. My side was turning white!

There could be only one reason for that; I must have been exposed to a distant death ray!

Nothing could be done; my life depended on how long I had been subjected to this murderous attack, and at what range. We had gone far that day, and I remembered stopping to rest in view of another group of hunters in the distance. Some member of that other band must have been responsible, but how had he recognized me at that distance?

After resting a mere ten minutes, an unusual restlessness had caused me to rise and walk away, and I had sat down again out of sight of the other party. What dim instinct had saved me? For had I remained, I should have become weak and dropped behind on the march, to fall an easy prey to some deadly beast of the forest. One learned to respect instincts in that land where life so often hung by a thread.

After some hours, the danger passed, but all the skin on that side peeled off, leaving me piebald until the hair grew again.

I spoke to nobody about this, though everybody could see what had happened. The more I thought about it, the more certain I became that the chief himself must have been behind the attack. It was common knowledge that he now regretted allowing Issa to come to me. He sent his attendants to her with an invitation to visit him in his cave, always unsuccessfully, and on the rare occasions when I saw him in the open air I could see the desire in his eyes when they rested on her.

She must have seemed very desirable to him, the only other women near being those hefty cave-women, who were as repulsive to him as they were to me.

I thought it over. The chief—I thought I understood him now—was being made rather ridiculous by the position, but would not do anything to make himself unpopular, such as openly killing me to steal my mate. But there were always secret ways, underhanded means. I could name several of the tribe who were secret agents of his. Clearly, if he wanted me out of the way, my days were numbered—if I remained with the tribe of Graypec.

About a week after my escape, I reached a decision. My side was almost healed. Having to lie on one side, I slept badly, and it was in the early hours of a chilly morning that I decided that the only hope for Issa or myself lay in flight. Her white body, now sun-tanned, bruised, and scratched by brambles, with the mop of hair making her look like a big, yellow doll, lay curled up on her heap of grass. The dim shapes of my father and his mate could hardly be seen in their end of the cavern, for dry weather had reduced the power of the waterfall, and there was a shortage of electricity for the lamps.

At my touch, her eyes opened. Dropping on my haunches beside her, I whispered that we were in danger here, and must flee. There was no need to say more. She knew as much as I, and I now shared the general fear of being heard, as though every stone held a secret microphone and some enemy listened to one's every word.

"To where?" she whispered. "My people would kill us both."

"Here is death for me, slavery for you."

At that she covered her face and cried.

"Whatever the dangers, we must face them," I urged. "Alive I can protect you; dead I cannot."

"But there is no life in the open, at night, for us," she returned, more calmly.

That was true. At the approach of darkness, a myriad of unseen things waited for the gathering dusk to give them a chance to pounce; but I urged that we must face it. Death before dishonor. Perhaps we could pass the nights in open spaces such as the cliff-top from which the dead sub-chief had shown me the island of the Larbies.

"Alas," she muttered, her voice muffled by dried grass, "I would go with you but I cannot—I—I shall soon bear you a child!"

Fool that I was not to have suspected it! Would this child be mine, Learoy Spofforth's, or would he be Kastrove's, the caveman? Could I expect it to inherit any qualities from Spofforth? It would be mine, yet not mine.

Her eyes were big and full of suffering. "Don't stay where you are in danger because of me," she said in a low tone, then quickly added: "That sounds as though I wanted to lose you. It would be fatal to go alone. Oh, I know not what to say."

I kissed her. "Keep smiling," I said; "you cannot go and I must stay with you. I must keep my eyes wide open, that's all." But I saw the rest of my life as a rope. It ran ahead for a short distance, then came to an end.

Weeks passed, but the chief held his hand. I saw him once when he was not aware of me; his eyes were on Issa, and they seemed to wear a calculating expression, as of one sure of his purpose and content to wait.

The birth of my child, a boy, marks in my mind the close of a period. It seems to foreshadow that other incident that turned my life upside down, the staggering prelude to a series of adventures that were to upset all my ideas of Kilsona, to take me among fantastic scenes and tremendous struggles, for objects I could barely conceive, to make me but a pawn in the play of vast forces, while I looked back on my life in the caves of Graypec as on some ideally happy picture.

Life on Kilsona had been fantastic, but in the main it had been understandable; now it was to become utterly bizarre, beyond comprehension.

I had no inkling of this in my mind as I held in my arms the tiny thing that was my child. The appearance of my son surprised and delighted me, for he was a perfectly normal boy such as any earth mother might be proud of, or so it seemed to me when I first saw him.

Afterwards I learned that when an ape-man mated with one of the townsfolk, such as Issa, the offspring was often a normal human being. It seems reasonable that two extremes should produce a medium-brutal strength and delicate weakness. The chief himself was a case in point.

To me it seemed wonderful. I even looked hopefully for signs of family resemblance, without much success. Very soon he began to bellow and to show a vigorous temper and a strong will. I suppose every inexperienced father, expecting a baby pictured as tiny, weak, and quiet, is surprised when the new arrival tries to dominate the whole family.

Issa cried because we had nothing but dried grass for him to lie on, and still more because it was impossible for her to keep him properly clean. She said he would die, but he thrived. I began to fear that the strain of nursing the voracious infant was draining her vitality, so strong was his appetite. I remarked about it to her.

"My people never nurse their children," she explained, "but what can I do? I can't get artificial food here."

There was no remedy. In agony, as the weeks passed, I watched her figure, which had filled out somewhat under the hard, healthy life, become more thin and pale until it seemed certain she must collapse. The mother was sacrificing her life for the child, and at times I was tempted to slay the baby that Issa might live.

Then came the incident that was to sweep all these problems aside.

Looking back, I cannot remember when I first knew that the Larbies were coming. The knowledge grew in the minds of the cavemen as the light of dawn slowly, imperceptibly grows in the night sky until the day is upon one. First was a vague uneasiness, then definite fear, then at last we all knew that on a certain day they would come. There was no announcement, no starting of a rumor, no one spoke about it; but in the minds of each, as though a thought-message had come to all, there grew with daily increasing clarity the knowledge that after so many days our rulers would be here.

It became increasingly plain that fear had laid its hand on the hearts of all. Voices were strangely hushed, all spring went out of the usually arrogant walk of the burly warriors, sub-chiefs became quiet and lost their tempers over trifles, heads drooped, and sly, fearful glances were cast from side to side. The chief hid in his cave.

When I had the time, between strenuous hunts and exhausted sleep, I puzzled myself greatly trying to think how it could be that these men, who should be bold and fearless, and were, should be in such a state of servitude. They had no fear of death—if courage were the chief of the virtues they were the chosen of heaven; yet here they went in crawling, abject fear of beings I had not seen, and who would not arrive for several days. It was not usual for them to look so far ahead.

They were of severely practical outlook, with slight traces of superstition, or even of religion, yet here they were in the grip of some dread that must be more than physical. It got on my nerves; more and more I began to see them as in the grip of a sort of disease, a mental parasite that had sunken horrible talons into the mind of each.

There were nights when I woke sweating, thinking I was caught in that grip myself.

"The tyranny of the mind," the dead leader had said, after leading me to the loneliest place he knew of, lest his words bring danger to me. At times, trembling with sympathy with those around, I imagined the Larbies as some huge, miraculous spider with the whole world of Kilsona in its fantastic grip.

Issa herself was in terror; she paid less heed to the cries of our son, lost appetite. It was an eerie business to see everybody quaking with unuttered terror, a feeling that even the babes shared in. In spite of my attempts at self-control, I started suddenly awake at night, crept around like a conspirator, and jumped at the slightest sound.

"This is foolishness," I told myself; "it can be nothing supernatural. Be calm."

"But you don't know," the instant thought flashed back at me, "you don't know *what* it is."

CHAPTER TEN

DAYS SLIPPED BY WITHOUT MY TAKING COUNT OF THEM. ONE morning I rose and, though I could see by the dim light that filtered along the passage that dawn had come, I was puzzled by the unnatural silence. Issa was curled up, awake, her eyes fixed and wide open. I felt subtly hurt that she made no appeal to me for comfort. My father and his mate crouched in their corner, taking no notice when I spoke to them.

The day had come! The unknown was upon us!

I wandered to the entrance, drew the bolts, and stood outside.

The usual guard of six warriors who sat around a fire in the open all night—I had several times been one of them, lest wild animals gained the rocky ledge above the black mouths of the caves and hurled stones down on us as we came out—was missing, and the fires were out. Yet no savage creature had taken advantage of their lapse; perhaps the very animals of the forest were held back by the mysterious influence of the rulers who were coming, and who, it seemed to me, had already filled the air around the cliff-face with a tingling creepiness, as of a strange electrical charge.

The red sun was rising clear of the distant hills to my left, through ragged clouds, some shot through with glorious reds and yellows, others darkly somber. The wind blew in sudden gusts, then, when one was sure it had quite gone and the day was breathless, it came again. An eerie silence was upon us; save for the soundless movement of the sun and clouds and the momentary stirring of leaves ruffled by the fitful breeze, all was still. No bird or insect flew in the air, no creeping thing stirred on the ground.

There was something there, something that brooded over the peaceful scene, something not of the sun, nor its growing, glorious dawn, nor of the forest, nor of the wide paths we had cut through the trees, nor of the space before me dotted with the ashes of dead fires, broken implements, and refuse-heaps, nor of the sandstone cliff behind me with its dark holes in which terrified people crouched, nor of the air that it filled with its brooding, sinister threat. I felt it in my creeping skin, my quivering nerves, my jerky breath.

The mouth of each occupied cave now held green heads that gazed tremblingly out. Alone of them all, I had ventured into the open. My courage failing me, I ran back to become one of four heads that filled the mouth of my own cave.

In spite of the height of the sun, now clear of the horizon and sending down golden shafts through the clouds, it was growing dark; yet scattered streaks of clouds in the blue sky and a faint blue mist, forecasting a hot day, in the distance, were all that could be seen to account for the gloom.

Presently I heard another sound, a blatant, piercing scream as of a steam-siren nearby. It shrilled out suddenly and violently, and seemed to come from the empty air in front of us. Many watchers threw themselves on the ground and hid their faces. Then came other sounds, among them the whirring of invisible propellers, the clanging of unseen doors, and the humming of masses of machinery.

"Mass hypnotism!" The idea leaped into my brain out of nothing. I felt I had struck on the explanation of the facts. I have heard the theory used to explain the famous Indian rope trick—the control of many minds by one man, so that they all think they see what is not there. Thus must my mind and those of all the people of Graypec now be controlled, either to cause us to hear things that were not there, or prevent us seeing the huge flying vessel resting on the ground in front of us—either that or the vessel must be totally invisible.

Looking carefully, I could see depressions in the sun-baked, hard-trodden ground where something very big and tremendously heavy rested. I strained my eyes. The dim, silvery outline of a huge oval ship, capable of carrying many hundred persons, was gradually taking shape.

Soon the shapes of opaque objects inside it cut off my view of the trees beyond. There was strange machinery, and there were indescribable, loathsome creatures that crawled sluggishly over smooth floors, horribly indistinct. Could these be the Larbies? A shiver passed through me, and I felt a spasm of horror such as I had not known since childhood. Soon these things were also hidden from view as the walls and partitions of the ship took form, hiding both the machines and the horrors that operated them.

I had had my first view of the Larbies, the ruling things of Kilsona, to whom all men on that world, save a small corner that still defied them, were slaves. I had expected to see men, or at the very worst, men-like beings, about as much like human beings as we know them as the men of Graypec were; but my brief glimpse had shown me that they had no relationship with humanity whatever.

They were mollusks, boneless creatures, their eyes on stalks and their bodies enclosed in horny shells like crabs.

In fact, of all earthly creatures, huge crabs are what they could most readily be likened to, though at times I think of them as gigantic lobsters. And they controlled delicate machines, ruled Kilsona!

The ship was plain enough now, concrete and solid. What I had glimpsed inside seemed now but a bad dream. In general appearance, the vessel was rather like one of those dirigible airships that were so frightfully expensive in money and in human lives in the early part of the century. But the sides of this vessel were of no thin canvas; they were of a smooth metal like untarnished aluminum, and the interior was divided into compartments by metal partitions. I had seen the ships of the Larbies many times, for ships like this one were common objects in our sky, as well as the smaller yellow flyers such as the one Issa had once flown.

"Come out!" Though I heard no sound, my brain received the peremptory order as though the words were barked in my ear. It was one of the remarkable powers of the Larbies that they could give their orders to any human being without making a sound. This, their power of making their ships invisible, and their mesmeristic qualities, I can explain only on the assumption of magic, or what amounts to the same thing, of scientific knowledge far beyond that possessed by man. A telephone is an instrument of magic, if you look at it in the right way.

Automatically, I made to step forward. Then I checked myself, asking, "Why have I been singled out like this?" What could those hidden beings want with me?

Anxiously I glanced around—to see the whole tribe shuffling out of the cave-mouths, heads hanging down. All had heard the order at the same time as I, and all moved to obey. We scrambled down the cliff with the unconscious ease of long practice, and walked to within ten feet of the ship, standing there on short legs and the palms of long arms, a grotesque line of motionless statues in the gloom between the cliff and the ship—an odd collection of worshippers in a queer cathedral. I had an unreasoning fear that the ship would roll upon and crush us.

For a while I felt that we were being inspected by unseen eyes, counted, examined. Then, "Where is your chief?" came again the telepathic demand.

Several seconds of waiting, then the door of the chief's cave opened with a crash and he strode stiffly out, an attendant on each side of him. Almost at the same instant a door in the side of the vessel opened, and a Larby came out to meet him.

It would be impossible to describe a Larby clearly in words unless I went to great length in doing so. I should need to be an artist to do the job properly. Imagine that a very bad artist saw for the first time in his life a crab and a lobster, then afterwards tried to draw them from memory, getting them badly mixed up. That was about what they looked like; they were of the color of mud, with many feelers and jointed legs. It was clear that they were beings whose natural home was the sea; only with difficulty were they maintaining themselves on dry land.

The one that now emerged was mounted on a square platform with pneumatic tires on the wheels, and driven by a neat little engine. There was another machine behind the mollusk, which seemed to me to be for the purpose of supplying the aerated water it needed for breathing, as a diver needs a supply of air. Down a sloping gangway ran the vehicle, closely followed by two others; then came a man walking behind them.

This man was tall and heavily built; he was dressed in rough, loose fitting clothes and had dull, stupid features like a well-fed domestic animal. From his self-important manner it might have been supposed that he was the commander of the vessel, but actually he was but the mouthpiece of his masters; his business was to make plain what they required of the tribe of Graypec.

They all halted a short way from the door of the ship, and the chief, waving back his attendants, came to meet them.

"Greetings, oh chief!" called the man from the ship in a loud, mechanical voice that echoed between the cliff and the side of the vessel.

"Greetings to our most gracious rulers!" boomed the chief in reply.

It was an impressive ceremony, designed to uphold the prestige of the chief in the tribe, and it showed me that the chief was but a puppet of the Larbies. I had a vision of all the tribes there must be of these green-haired cavemen on Kilsona, each tribe under a master chosen by these things from the sea.

"Your health, oh chief?"

"It continues to be excellent."

All this was routine procedure, but now the visitors became more business-like.

"Your numbers are?"

The reply came at once: 55 adult males, 66 females, making 121 full-grown. Cubs over one year, 40 males, 47 females. 35 infants under one year, making a total of 243. There are also one captive yellow woman and two crossbreeds, myself and one male infant. Grand total, therefore, 246."

"A male infant cross-breed. Excellent! He shall be taken and trained as a chief." (I felt myself grow hot and cold, and Issa stiffened beside me on hearing that our child was to be taken from us.) "Your total strength is six more than your allocation."

"But 21 less than a year ago."

There was a pause while the interpreter bent and appeared to communicate with the creature on the middle platform.

"Such a big drop is strange. There has been no exceptionally severe weather, and we took only eighteen warriors from you on the last occasion. How do you account for it?"

"Hunting accidents, gracious one. We were told on your last visit that our numbers were too many, and ordered to cut down our cultivated area by half." (I jumped at this, for some of the food of the tribe was supplied by roots and berries that grew, as I thought, wild; and I had unsuccessfully tried to show them how to increase crops by drainage, clearing away brambles, etc.) "This has made more hunting necessary, and so reduced the numbers of the game, throwing a still heavier burden on the warriors of the tribe."

"As it was meant to do," the man said sharply. "Still, 21 in a year is too big a drop. Reclaim one third of the disused area. Anything special to report; any cases of unruliness?"

"One only."

"Bring him forward!"

The two personal servants of the chief must have crept, unnoticed, up behind me, for on these words they seized me by the wrists and throat and propelled me out of the line. I heard a moan from Issa.

"Details," the man demanded.

"General attitude of disrespect, asks repeated questions, unlawful meddling with food-crops. Very bad case, gracious one."

"Put him on the platform. He shall be one of the quota of soldiers from your tribe for this year."

I was gripped by three men who had appeared from nowhere. They had pistols of a strange pattern in holsters at their sides, and whips with wire thongs under their arms. They hustled me up a railed metal staircase in the side of the ship, and onto a platform some twenty feet above the ground. It would have been madness to resist, and before I realized what they were doing, they had fastened my ankles together with a brassy chain a foot long. From here I could see all that happened below, but I could not get down.

Then this was what the chief had been waiting for—to get rid of me so that he might force himself on Issa! When I looked down at her and saw that the poor girl, deprived at once of her child and her husband, had collapsed on the stony ground, an animal fury surged up in me, and had it been possible to climb over the rails that kept me on the platform, I would have sprung to the ground and nothing could have prevented me from smashing in the chief's face. But the chain held me back, and the fence, small of mesh and sloping inwards, was difficult to climb.

"We need another eleven fighters," declared the man who did the talking for the Larbies.

The chief pointed to eleven of his followers in turn, cavemen and cave-women, and each one picked out shuffled forward and mounted the stairs to the platform, to lie on his or her face, moaning softly or shaking with fear. I noticed that the chief, who might have lessened the trouble by always picking husband and wife together, left a sorrowing mate behind for each of the eleven. As I watched, I saw how he was choosing them; he was ridding himself of everybody who had shown any signs of independence of thought, of moral courage.

"When are we likely to return?" I asked a comrade in distress.

"You know there is no return for us," came the answer. "We are as ones already dead."

Issa, Issa! In my agony, my soul reached out to her. Did she perceive it? I think she did, for at that very moment she jumped to her feet and ran forward, calling out: "Take me also! Take me also! You have taken my man and my child; take me too!"

At the bidding of the chief, his servants seized her.

"Stay!" called the interpreter, sharply. Whatever one may say of the Larbies, they possessed boundless intelligence, and the motives of the chief must have been perfectly obvious to them. "If she wishes to come, let her come. One extra will not matter."

I almost laughed aloud. How I wished I could have been on the ground instead of so far above, so that I might have seen the beaten chief's face, have enjoyed his efforts to hide his anger! The next moment Issa was beside me, and we embraced. But we were bound for an unknown destination, our child was somewhere inside the ship, and we knew not whether we should ever see him again.

Then came the last act of this annual tragedy. Every child under a year old was brought from the caves and carried to the ship. Some wept, some ran away, and they seemed very lively and noisy with their elders so quiet.

The three Larbies on their automatic platforms and their human servant drew back towards the ship; I thought they had gone inside, for they were now hidden from me, then I heard these words in a metallic voice I had not heard before.

"We go now," it chanted. "Remember that the Larbies are wise, good and all-powerful. Repeat after me, all of you: *To he who thinks disrespectfully of the Larbies shall be everlasting torment, torment that shall endure after death and forevermore!*"

And the whole tribe on the ground repeated, some gruffly, shrilly, some slowly, some quickly:

"To he who thinks disrespectfully of the Larbies, shall be everlasting torment, torment that shall endure after death and forevermore!"

The door clanged; the ship rose. One by one we entered the vessel through the door before us, all of us knowing that we had seen the caves of Graypec for the last time; and of what lay ahead, we knew nothing.

CHAPTER ELEVEN

OUR ACCOMMODATION ABOARD THE SHIP OF THE LARBIES, which was taking us to the perpetual wars of Kilsona, was crude and simple in the extreme. We were housed like cattle.

The thirteen of us were tightly packed in one large room, with a long trough such as one associates with pigsty's at the forward end, and a curious arrangement fixed to the wall whereby a bowl of drinking water was kept half full and never spilled, no matter how the ship tilted. There was an immediate rush for this, and it was a long time before one could obtain a drink without first joining in a pushing, quarrelling crowd.

No other arrangements of any sort were made for us. The door onto the outside platform was locked, and we were unable to leave our single compartment. Well was it for Issa that she was by now well accustomed to foul smells and unsanitary conditions, but I grieved that I could do nothing to improve things. Fortunately, when the ship went fast, a constant stream of chilly fresh air blew into the room.

Now that what they thought to be the worst of all possible fates had befallen us, the cavemen became, oddly enough, quite lively and cheerful. Reaction set in from their first despair, and our animal energy found an outlet in violent horseplay. We rolled and tumbled and played at fighting, quite forgetting where we were. Our glorious health—we were the pick of the tribe—would not let us remain miserable for long. Some, resigning themselves to the loss of their mates, began advances towards making fresh attachments, and soon there were three couples mated and absolutely ignoring the extraordinary publicity of their domestic arrangements.

Others reacted differently, and became talkative. From fragmentary answers, I pieced together the facts that these visits of the Larbies to the caves of Graypec happened in the fall of every year, and always a number of young adults were taken away, and all infants under a year old. After several weeks, the infants were returned, but the adults never returned. Naturally the returned cubs could not say where they had been; but I gathered that they seemed cowed, as though some of their natural spirit had been taken out of them.

Never did I learn what happened to these kidnapped cubs; but on that point I have formed a guess, a guess that all my experience of Kilsona seems to support. If I have not hit on the truth, then the actual facts must be very like my conjecture. If correct, my guess would explain why the cavemen and the men of the crystal cities like Teth-Shorgo were in such complete subjection to the Larbies, never so much as thinking of opposing their wishes, still less of rising and throwing off the hideous yoke.

In my view, the Larbies were expert hypnotists; they had studied hypnotism as a science, and had carried it to such a state of perfection that they were able to keep whole nations under their control by its means. Now no person can be hypnotized who is unwilling to be; but we all know how strong hypnotic suggestion can be, once control of the subject's mind has been obtained. But the Larbies might establish their control over the minds of their subjects during the first year of life. When grown up and capable of resisting, the damage would be done, for their minds would already be in chains. I seemed to see the helpless babes lying in rows while expert Larbies handled complicated machines with wires running to each little head, impressing on it the suggestions that would make it forever after the helpless subject of the will of the Larbies.

So smooth was our flight that we did not seem to be moving, except when we listened to the rush of wind past the walls of the ship. There was a mild rising and falling, like a gentle swell at sea. I believe we were driven by two beams of power that strode the earth like enormously long legs, but here again I am guessing. The propellers were small, and used, I think, for steering only.

In one wall was a wide window through which, had there been nothing on my mind, I might have enjoyed the endless variety of scenery—untamed by man—that flowed swiftly past.

"My home town," said Issa, pointing.

We were approaching Teth-Shorgo, which I had not noticed because it seemed to be built entirely of a sort of green glass cloudily transparent and hard to detect among the trees. Taking a longer dip than usual, the ship settled down towards it like some huge bird of prey.

"We are going to land," I cried; "perhaps they will return you to your people."

Crazy optimist that I was! Even then I did not know that Kilsona was a world of hate, all mercy crushed out of its people by grim, endless struggles. I had never believed that Issa would be made to fight; but I was to learn that women on this world got no more consideration than men. We warriors from the caves of Graypec and the more civilized people of Teth-Shorgo, men and women, were mere fodder for the wars with the Gorlemites—helpless slaves without rights.

Looking down on Teth-Shorgo, I was startled to see what a big place it once had been, a rough oval in shape built on the estuary of a river (of which river the stream that ran through Graypec was a tributary). It had been fifteen miles wide by twenty long. But now most of it was deserted; plants had found root in layers of dust, to provide a footing for larger plants in their rotting remains, until trees came and their roots and stems pushed aside walls and tore up roads by the force of their growth. The forest was fighting to win back its lost territory, smashing, covering all with dead leaves and grass, and spreading itself, exultant, above the ruins. Here and there a solitary wall or a round roof remained to show where the streets had once been.

The part still in use, about two square miles, north of the river, sufficed to show that the ancient architects had done their work well. Where a big building remained intact it always showed a pleasing shape with rounded, not pointed, roof; and where all was not covered with dust or soot it could be seen that the builders had worked beautiful effects in the contrasting colors of the translucent stone that was their chief material. A wonderful place it must once have been, not a chimney in view and even the factories things of delicate beauty.

In the center of the part of the town that was still in use was a railed park. The grass was patchy and neglected, but it provided a perfect landing place, and towards this we settled down.

The door to the outside platform was opened, and I went outside with Issa. My ankles were unchained.

Curiously I looked about the streets, but all the inhabitants near were hiding from us. When they began to creep out, one by one, from corners and doorways, I saw that they were slender, semi-nude, white-skinned and had mops of yellow hair.

Our landing was quiet, and I began to hope that these people, so much more human looking than the cave dwellers, were not under the same cruel domination as they were.

"Oh, we are," said Issa, shuddering, when I asked her. "Don't speak about it again, please."

Bells chimed in the town, announcing our arrival, and a highly decorated auto drove up, and three Larbies with three men who seemed to be their personal servants were whirled away in it along the streets.

Getting up from where I had been lying looking over the edge of the platform, I turned to Issa. Here was her home; here were her people. The stairway was open and no guards could be seen. Why did she not slip away into the city and escape? But though I argued that now was her chance to escape, I could not persuade her to take the step; the barrier of suggestion in her mind was too strong for me to break down.

Our companions from Graypec came running and tumbling down the steps like boys out of school, and told us that the guards had given us permission to stretch our legs in the park provided we did not go over the railings.

Going down with them and taking a closer look at the sightseeing inhabitants of the crystal city, I found them less attractive than they had looked from a distance. They had a deceitful look, and their slack, full mouths gave them a sensuous appearance, that, along with their weak, puny bodies, made them unpleasant to look at. Had I been obliged to live among them, I should have feared treachery, a cowardly stab in the back. Their faces were thickly painted to achieve an artificial, exaggerated beauty.

I heard strains of music, and thinking that this might be their redeeming feature, I moved towards the sounds. It was a long time since I had heard any real music; but I was again disappointed, for it was merely a shrill female voice and a coarse male one singing a ballad of indescribable lewdness.

Around them, the crystal buildings, with their sweeping beauty and symmetry of design, were a marked contrast to the men and women who moved among them. The houses were dirty and neglected and many were falling to pieces—the product of another age that built well with good, durable materials.

"The flower of humanity tottering to its final ruin," I muttered. A deep sadness filled me.

Missing Issa, I looked around to find her curled up and lying on the damp grass, a miserable, weeping heap. I went to her quickly.

"I went away from the other slaves and you," she said, "to ask if any of the people of the city would tell my father that I was here and would like to see him. They came to me with smiles, then, when close enough they—they spat on me."

As I bent to raise her, I heard sneering remarks that can be paraphrased as, "She is his—she belongs to an ape-man."

Secretly, I picked up several rocks from the overgrown path, then hurled them with all my strength over the railings at the mockers, upon which they fled. Several replied with handfuls of filth from the roadway.

Maddened with rage, I hurled stone after stone, some small, some large, some rebounding from the railings while others smashed or bounced off roadway or sidewalk to bring down a tinkle of glass from broken windows. And soon I was not alone in this, for the other cavemen had seen that a fight was going on and rushed to join in. Very quickly I had many helpers who, forgetting all else, alternately threw rocks or uttered their low, deep war cry; for I had unknowingly stirred deep, racial hatreds. A merry battle was soon raging.

Not long was this brawl allowed to proceed unchecked, for soon the strident scream of a steam-siren smote through the air. At the sound, the people of the city forgot the battle and turned to flee, pursued by shouts of triumph from the cavemen, who had been outnumbered but whose powerful muscles had enabled them to throw the stones with damaging effect. Then the cause of the panic was seen, a group of men strode along the sidewalk, guns in one hand and whips in the other, slashing the remaining rioters into subjection. Two of them were shot dead as they ran away. In a little while the streets were clear.

But we inside were not allowed to escape without punishment for our part in the affair, for five men appeared on our side of the fence, similarly armed, and began to lay about them freely. Though the wire-like thongs of their whips cut like knives, the proud warriors of Graypec would have fought back till the last one died, had not the fear of the Larbies, whose tools these were, fallen on the hearts of us all. None of us was permanently injured, for we had value as slaves and were to die in the wars, but many of us carried long scars from that day as long as we lived. We had had our first taste of the disciplinary methods of our masters.

I had seen enough of Teth-Shorgo, the beautiful city erected by men of long ago whose repulsive progeny, these sub-men, lived in sloth and filth among the fading glories their ancestors had labored to erect.

Hearing a loud clang, and seeing my companions drifting around to the main entrance of the flying vessel, I saw an automobile run down the gangway drawing behind it a cage on wheels; and inside it were the thirty-six infants who had been taken from the caves of Graypec. All wept lustily, from hunger it seemed, and amongst them the white skin of my own son showed clearly. At the sight I ran forward, intending to drag the driver out of the car and recover my son; but burning lashes wrapped themselves around my body, drowning all things in a welter of searing pain, and at a guttural command several arms seized me and pulled me back. Dimly I was aware that other parents had also dashed forward, to receive similar punishment for their love for their children.

Then we were all penned in our single room again, or rather, stable, and we continued our journey. Two of the men with whips and guns visited us now and then, and from these we learned that we were now bound for the wars.

Steadily the ship went on its way for hundreds of miles, until the increasing vigor of the vegetation, making the land exotic with beautiful flowers, showed that we were nearing the tropics. Then a narrow sea, dotted with islands, passed by, and we were over a great desert of shifting, sun-baked sand. It made me think of crossing the Mediterranean and coming on the hot, parched Sahara.

Could it be in this desert that the age-long struggle was being waged? As we settled down near a cluster of crude stone buildings not far from the sea, I scanned the horizon for signs of fighting, the flash of guns, moving figures, or even, possibly, a beleaguered city, but there was nothing but the endless sand.

Some message must have been received from below, for we did not land but recovered our height and, after hovering for a while, set off silently across the desert. As we went, I noticed a low whine rapidly ascending the musical scale until it was too high to be audible; then suddenly there was no ship about me, nothing but air and the pitiless sun above and the hot sands below. Yet I could still feel the solid floor beneath my feet and hear the startled cries of the cavemen around me whom I could not see. Issa's voice asked if I were still there.

The ship was invisible! Somehow the Larbies had achieved the task of causing the whole ship to vibrate at a rate so rapid that light rays passed right through it, as though it were more transparent than glass.

This invisibility was not perfect, for small objects had an uncanny way of appearing and vanishing again. This happened when anything was dropped, for while it was falling, it was momentarily free from vibrations. Besides this, the shadowy parts of weird machinery showed, per-haps because their motions set up vibrations of their own that interfered with those producing invisibility; and also there were a number of dark spheres in which I believe the Larbies shielded themselves from the effects of invisibility, for these effects were unpleasant. After about an hour, one began to feel persistent aches throbbing through every bone and sinew of one's body. How far this was due to the high-frequency vibrations, and how much of it was caused by the unhindered passage of the ultraviolet light through one's tissues, I cannot say.

We were now rushing over the desert at the greatest speed we had yet reached. Beneath us passed green spots that marked occasional oases, and once I saw the half-buried ruins of a crystal city. Nowhere was there a sign of life.

A sharp whine sounded through the air, exactly as though some heavy missile had been fired at us; then came another. The sands looked empty of anything that might have shown hostility, and surely the very little of the ship that could be seen was not enough to make a target; yet those shots were undeniable. I saw and heard the bursting of the shells after they passed us.

Pausing not an instant in their flight, the beings in charge of the vessel emitted two bursts of flame from somewhere behind, bursts that were followed by loud explosions on the ground below. It was, I know now, mere blind shooting hurting nobody, mutual greetings, as it were; and without troubling any more about our unseen foes, we left them far behind.

Such was our first taste of war. It was very different from what I had imagined war would be like with such powerful beings as the Larbies engaged in it. The death rays had impressed me so much that I had pictured opposing fleets of airplanes wiping each other out with beams of them—and great cities sheltering under dome-like screens of defensive force, striking back with flashes of destruction against attackers who sought to wear down the screen by sheer power.

All this is how wars of the future are described by writers of fiction, but if my experiences on Kilsona are any guide, this is all wrong. The Larbies had all the rays, heat - rays, death rays, and disintegration rays that writers are so fond of, but they seldom used them because they were so wasteful of power, and a crumb of their highly efficient explosives would usually do all that was wanted.

"Look, the great blue eye!" Issa interrupted my reverie.

Following the direction of her pointing arm, I saw across the desert, miles away, a spot of blue light that came and went in rapid throbs about as rapidly as the fastest the human eye can blink. The sun was setting, and as we made towards the light, the surrounding sands were lit by the light of the winking glow. On the summit of a granite mountain that lifted its worn head thousands of feet above the desert stood a round stone building bearing a pillar at the top of which a large globe shone, first bright blue, then pale violet, changing several times a second.

On the lower slopes of the mountain, and around its base, the land was green with verdure, making a ring of cultivated ground with the mountain in the center. Beyond that the sea of sand resumed its sway.

Visible once more, we landed on a level space where a massive step had been cut in the rock. Here we were ordered to descend, and were hustled through an opening into a spacious cavern hewn out of the rock. It was a huge cave, the smooth floor, ice-cold to our feet after the heat outside, reflecting our bodies with clarity, and looking unsafe to walk on. The walls and the roof, however, were of the natural rough rock.

Into the interior of the mountain we shuffled, the Larbies going ahead on their automatic wheeled platforms, while a dozen armed guards marched behind us. As we went on, every cough or grunt echoed and re-echoed from the walls. Issa's pale face was drawn, and I myself was shivery with fear, but I noticed that the slaves from Graypec had recovered something of their natural confidence. After all, they had lived in caves all their lives; there was nothing to be afraid of in a cave—it was not like great flying-ships that vanished from sight while one was inside of them.

Presently our passage ran into a still larger cavern, so great that the farther side was lost in the gloom, and most of the floor was occupied by a lake of cold, still water. With a sharp splash, the leading Larby left his moving platform and plunged headlong into the water, followed by the others. I suppose they must have been glad to get back to what were their natural conditions; their platforms remained standing in a line at the edge of the lake.

Our guards directed us along a narrow path that skirted the lake. Looking up, I saw a patch of star-strewn sky above our heads; the cavern was open to the heavens, as though it were the crater of an extinct volcano. Idly, I wondered where the water came from, to be so far above the level of the arid desert, how deep the pool was, whether the hole went on down like a dagger wound in the earth, or whether it reached to underground seas—and whether it was a mere resting place for the disgusting things from the sea who had brought us here, or whether they had whole towns and villages in those depths. Most of these questions I cannot answer, but I know there were vast hidden lakes far under the desert, and an odd idea has come to me that perhaps the very first Larbies were bred in these dark, stagnant waters, so far under the ground. Yet they could see, and neither bright light nor moderate heat ever seemed to trouble them much.

We came now to another cavern where a score of armed guards stood around like statues. Have I mentioned that all these caves were lighted by electric globes set in niches in the walls? Here we were grouped in the middle of the floor, and a thin, dried-up man inspected us. For an instant he looked puzzled as his eyes rested on Issa, but he took no further notice of her. He began to address us in a high-pitched, cracked voice.

"I know you are all tired and hungry," he began. "When I have done with you, you will be allowed to eat and rest. I suppose you all know why you are here; this desert that surrounds us is the desert of Gorlem and it is the abode of the murderous beings you have heard of as the men of Gorlem, who seek to destroy all other men on Kilsona. It is our wise and beneficent rulers, the Larbies, whom we have to thank that so far they have been prevented from carrying out their dastardly plans. In this struggle, and it is our struggle as well as theirs, they need our aid, and you have all been specially picked out for the honor of defending your homes, your children, and your mates from these terrible beings.

"In this you will not be left to your own resources, which alone would be of little avail against our foes, but you will have the benefit of the unfathomable wisdom of our rulers, and you will be provided with weapons and with means of living in the desert. That is why you have been brought here, to be trained in the use of these weapons before you go into action. Your training will last for a period of several weeks, during which time you will be comfortably housed and looked after in a training establishment on the edge of this settlement.

"One other point I have to mention is discipline; this war cannot be carried on without discipline. The soldier who will not obey orders implicitly is a danger to his fellows. Therefore, if any of you are stubborn or make yourselves difficult to instruct, you must expect no mercy. The first step in your training commences now. All of you will look steadily at the mirrors over my head."

While the apologist was speaking, two of his colleagues had wheeled in a tall frame on which four large rounded mirrors were arranged in a circle. As we looked at them, these mirrors began to revolve, catching and reflecting the many lights on the walls in dazzling flashes.

I stiffened. The optical effects of rapidly revolving mirrors are sometimes used by hypnotists as a mechanical aid to help in putting subjects into a sleep in which they are under control. We were being put through that process again!

I sensed a shudder running through the whole group of slaves, and several moaned with fear. So rapidly came the reflected flashes that they seemed to hold my gaze riveted. I wanted to close my eyes but could not do so. Faster and faster they went, and now I understood how the cavemen were held in such helpless subjection; for the influence was beginning to affect me, though I steeled myself against it.

As I watched the rapid changes of the mirrors, I seemed to be losing all power of ordered thought, to be drifting into a trance-like dream. Memories were rising out of the past, memories that belonged to Kastrove the caveman, slave of the Larbies. Long, long ago I had seen such flashing mirrors, and they had stamped on my brain a record, a series of facts never to be questioned. Now they were going over them again, reaffirming their teachings. Before I could speak, before I could walk, I had watched such mirrors, and they had burned their lessons into my brain as with a branding iron. They were sacred beyond all things, and if I ever doubted them, or their makers, the Larbies, I should be guilty of treachery to the deepest things of life, established before the first man drew breath; and then my punishment would be more than death, it would endure without end, after my body had rotted away, and I should be a traitor, banded to all eternity.

All this poured into my mind, not as something being told to me, but as something I had always known, and of which I was now being reminded. It was like some deep, intense religion, to which I must always be ready to be sacrificed, and its Gods were the Larbies.

I seemed to be two different men at the same time, and while one was whole-heartedly accepting this horrible tyranny of the soul, the other was a calm, detached background, saying that I must resist, that this was but the voice of creatures whose real purpose was to destroy mankind, and that I must preserve my freedom of mind if I were still to call myself a man.

All was profoundly still, save for the turmoil in my mind, then from beside me, startling me horribly, came the voice of Issa. She spoke in a clear, cold voice, resounding through the cavern in the granite rock, the slow voice of one who speaks against her will.

"I would not say it," she began, mechanically, lifelessly, addressing no one, "but I must. There is an enemy amongst us now; a man of Gorlem. I would not declare it were it not sinful to be silent, for he is my own mate!"

I knew at once that my death warrant had been uttered. I had forgotten that Issa believed me, for reasons I did not understand, to be a man of Gorlem, a belief strengthened by my knowledge of things unknown to either the cavemen of Graypec or Issa's own people of the crystal cities; and now she spoke and condemned me.

None of the slaves around us spoke or moved. I doubt if they heard, or even if Issa herself knew what she had said. A calm voice, impersonal as a tolling bell, sounded in answer.

"We already knew, for he was resisting the control. It is well for you that you spoke, or you would have shared his fate."

The shock had shaken me wide-awake, but there was no hope of even making a fight for life, for many guns were aimed at me. I stepped out from my place, for I had no wish to hide behind the bodies of others. It is unpleasant to wait for death, to be full of health and vigor and yet unable to struggle; but a queer sense of the unreality of it all had come over me. I did not think I should die so soon. Probably every condemned criminal thinks he is not really going to die, that at the last moment a reprieve or something will come to save him.

One of the armed guards produced a coil of thin rope, and they began, without a word, to tie my arms and legs together. Idly I wondered why they should take so much trouble when it would have been simpler to shoot me where I stood, or stick one of their sharp knives into me.

The thongs that held my arms passed in front of my body, so that there was not the slightest hope of my releasing myself. Then they carried me out of the cavern along the passage that led to the water-filled crater. I saw reflected in the calm surface the many lights set in niches in the walls of rock, and the gap, far above, through which a few stars shone, then I had been hurled out far across the water, and the splash of my body set the reflections dancing.

As I sank, I wished I had fought in the hall of the mirrors, had faced an explosive pellet rather than the slow death I was doomed to now. To be bound hand and foot, unable to move, until one's little supply of air is exhausted, waiting till one *must* breathe, then getting lungs and stomach full of water, seemed a most unpleasant end.

How far I went down, I cannot say. As a boy, unable to swim, I once got out of my depth and was finally pulled out almost unconscious. It had seemed to me then that I sank down, mile after mile, while time slowly dragged itself out, hour after hour. In just the same way, I seemed to go down, down for miles now, while time mercilessly drifted on. Something struck me spitefully in the side; I think it was a jagged point of rock, but it may have been a fish.

It took a long time to drown a green-haired ape-man because of those reservoirs of oxygen in their bodies; but even this must be exhausted in time; I must drown in the end. A steady tugging at my ankles told of the weights tied there to make sure that I should sink.

There was a faint light in the water around me, a light that did not filter down from above but had its origin here in the depths. Then, in this light, I saw something coming towards me, a thing of feathery arms, pointed claws, and horny jaws—a Larby! I was afraid of it and tried to make myself smaller, to hide from its stalked eyes.

I was still able to think lucidly, and I reflected that probably the reason why I had been thrown into the lake was so that the Larbies would find me at the bottom, and deal with me as they thought fit.

This one came towards me, took off the weights, and towed me along behind itself. Puzzled, I could only think that I was being dragged into some hidden lair to be devoured at leisure.

For a while all was dark as we went on our way; then, strangely enough, I was lifted up, *out of the water,* and placed on a flat, wet surface. Here I lay like a trussed fowl.

Light came suddenly, lights above me, lights in the water below me. I was on a sort of table inside a sort of diving bell, and all around were Larbies and weird machines. As boys catch crabs and put them in jars of water to examine them, so these huge intelligent crabs kept me in a jar of air and watched me. One reached under the edge and injected into my neck something that had a freezing effect like the novocaine a dentist uses on one's gums. Thereafter my thoughts were very vague.

Jostling figures moved about me; lights of many colors danced before my eyes. I had an impression of enormous beings who probed my brain with streaks of violet light that burned like red-hot needles, of being dropped from a height, of being spun rapidly around until all was whirling confusion. Later I was mixed up in a great machine in which such familiar things as cogwheels, electric motors, shafts and pistons, were working together, interlocking, with bewildering things that defied all the laws of dynamics.

A terrific explosion occurred in my brain, blowing me into microscopic fragments.

I was a tiny creature pinned to a board alone in the desert under the sun, and a rolling, reverberating voice was thundering questions at me.

"Who are you?"

I replied that I was a caveman from the tribe of Gray-pec.

A spasm of sheer agony swept through me.

"That is not true. I know from your reactions that is not true."

I began to tell my story, not expecting to be believed. As I did so I could feel the astonishment produced by my words. Then I was asked questions on scientific matters, but of course I could give only the most indefinite answers to these. I am no scientist.

"Do not play with me. Answer the question!"

I tried to.

"Silence, fool! It is true, you know nothing. I thought you were trying to deceive me."

"A queer insect," I thought I heard one Olympian deity say to another.

"Yes, but harmless," was the answer. Thereafter I slept peacefully for a long time.

CHAPTER TWELVE

AT LAST I AWOKE FROM THIS NIGHTMARE TO FIND MYSELF lying in a shed of rough wooden planks, feeling as though I had been cut into pieces and hastily stuck together again. One of the armed guards was holding under my nose a bottle from which came a strong smell like sal-volatile. I was given a lump of raw meat and an iron jug full of water.

At first I shrank from the food, but gradually hunger came back. There were about fourteen slaves here, both cavemen and women and people from cities, such as Teth-Shorgo, and all of them had thrown themselves down as though exhausted. Each one, like myself, was tethered by a brassy chain to a wooden pillar. All were strangers to me.

Moving from one to another, the guards shook them awake and placed meat and water in front of each.

There was a weight around my neck, which I discovered when it flapped on my chest when I sat up. Each of the other occupants of that barn, I saw, was wearing a similar ornament, a coppery disk with markings cut into it, on a bright, yellow chain. Identification tabs! Now I knew that indeed we were slaves.

Eating, I tried to piece together my confused recollections of the night. The Larbies now knew all there was to know about me; of that I was certain. Yet, insultingly, instead of treating me as a civilized man, entitled to courteous treatment, or even as a dangerous enemy, they regarded me with contempt. I did not so much mind their calling me "useless," but to be called "harmless" stung—though perhaps it was lucky for me that they did think so.

And now I was herded with other slaves to be trained to fight for them in a war in which my sympathies were, as far as I had any, on the other side. Yet I knew nothing about the enemy yet; it might be they were as dangerous as we were told they were.

Where was Issa, and why was I in a group of strangers?

The guards were making us rise and walk out through the door into the open. The glare of the sun was dazzling.

I spoke to one man, but his eyes were dull and hopeless, and he made no reply. Several others I tried, only to be met with the same despair, the same lack of interest in life. A sharp-eyed guard saw me talking to them, and expressed his disapproval by striking at me with his many-thonged whip. I had felt these whips before, in the park at Teth-Shorgo, and I made a desperate twist to avoid the force of the stroke. I suffered several sore lines across my back in spite of that, and looking up at him from under my arm, I resolved to revenge myself at the first chance I got. He had bloated, blotched cheeks, a broad nose, and eyes almost hidden under thick folds of flesh.

Pitilessly intense, the sun shone down, making the distant view hazy where the air quivered in the heat. We were on the very edge of the settlement, the barren desert in front and the mountain dominating all behind. The great blue light still pulsed in its tower on the apex.

Another group of slaves was approaching, and I thrilled to recognize my neighbors from the caves of Graypec, the "discipline" they had been subjected to being plainly shown by their weary air and, when one of them turned around, by deep lacerations where whip-lashes had cut his back. On the neck of each one was an identification tab.

Issa passed close to me, and with one eye on the guard I called to her softly; but her eyes, like those of the others, were fixed straight ahead in unwinking, trance-like stare, as though she neither saw nor heard. Fortunately, she had not been disfigured by whip marks; the yellow-haired people were not treated with the same roughness as the cavemen and women.

It was then that I had my first introduction to the light sand tanks I was to become so familiar with. At first glance I took them for shallow mounds of sand, but on close inspection they proved to be sort of covered-in motorcars designed for running across desert country unnoticed. They were low and wide, casting no shadows, and their edges, hinged to cope with uneven surfaces, ran on rollers. Riders and engines were completely concealed, so that from a distance it was practically impossible to distinguish them from the surrounding sand, unless it happened to be a different color from the dull yellow of the cars.

Flaps were opened in the backs of these vehicles, and into each of them one of us clambered, followed by an armed guard. Inside of mine there was room for several persons, seats in which one sat with one's feet straight out before one and looked out through peep-holes, plank benches for sleeping on, and cupboards for food and water. I had wondered how motorcars could run over sand without the wheels sinking in, but I saw now that instead of wheels these cars had endless belts to run on, what are called caterpillar tracks, like those used in tanks in our own wars.

The guard who had climbed in after me began to give me instructions in driving the car, a series of simple rules I was made to learn by heart. Like so many tortoises with hidden legs, the other cars slid silently and rapidly away from the yard, and I was told to follow. Under the eye of my trainer, I sent the strange car racing over the desert, first the hard-packed sand near the settlement, then the looser sand farther away, where our car left wide tracks behind it. Once I was told to go straight across a dune, or hill of sand, and the car went over it easily, though our speed was reduced. I learned to stop, to start, to turn right and left, and the great blue light became a tiny speck in the distance. There was a curious instrument in front of me; it was like a clock lying on its back, and I noticed that no matter how I turned the car, the hour hand always pointed to the mountain and the blue globe, something like a compass.

Naturally, it did not take me long to learn how to manage this simple vehicle, and my trainer was well satisfied with the progress I made. "You're a quick learner," he stated. "Better than most I've had. Some never learn, die under the whip before they'll learn. I was told you were something unusual, and I was to keep a sharp eye on you, but I see no reason why you should not make a good soldier."

He took a flask from a cupboard and drank out of it, wiping his mouth with the back of his hand afterwards.

"I'm as tired of this as you are, monkey," he said. "Follow my directions and I'll take you where we can have a rest. Only keep your mouth shut about it afterwards, mind."

Very readily, I undertook to keep his secret, for the heat was very trying, and he guided me to an oasis where there was a pool of water and feathery palm trees that gave a delightful shade. Here I sat chained to my seat while he first swam in the lake and then sat in the shade and drank.

Hours later, half drunk, he staggered back into the car and mumbled something, upon which I set off across the desert trusting to the steady guidance of the hour hand in the clock face, which became luminous when the sun sank.

"Good work, monkey," was the only observation my trainer made on the way, except to tell me to go slowly, we were early.

It was morning when we arrived, and my body was stiff and sore from sitting so long in one position, but when I saw the bleeding backs of the others, where "discipline" had been invoked, I realized that I was getting off very lightly. I now felt glad of my quickness at learning, and of the drunken habits of my particular trainer.

Our instructions were carried on for many days, as the man in the mountain had said; but in my own case, I was soon doing nothing but taking my overseer straight to his oasis and back. The place was not unknown, for as other pupils became proficient, they appeared at the oasis with their teachers. In the night we kept to the cars for warmth, and wore thick cloaks.

My only anxiety was for Issa. I pictured her alone with one of these bullies, and the thought tortured me. But when I saw that all women were taught by females, I was more contented. She noticed me now, and smiled at me when we passed, she going in and I coming out, so that I assumed she was now enjoying the easier time of one who had qualified. It was another group that came out as I went in, for there were three "gangs," two always training while a third slept.

About three weeks passed and nothing more happened; I was lulled into a false security. Then one morning I woke suddenly, full of a feeling that something was wrong. It was, I judged, not quite an hour before I should be roused to take the car out again; yet I knew, quite simply and clearly, that Issa was in trouble. So clear and definite was the knowledge that I did not stop to wonder how I knew it.

I got to my feet and looked about the barn. Shining through many cracks and knotholes in the roof, the sun sprinkled the gloom with golden streaks and dots of light.

That was it, I could see now; the place was *emptier* than it had been. Counting the sleeping forms I found that there were nine only. When I had first come to this place there had been fourteen. What had happened to the other five?

There was one, a stoutish, very stupid youth who had suffered terribly under the lashes; I could guess what his fate had been, poor fellow. But the other four?

In the open I had sometimes seen what looked like wrecked sand-cars, but I had not been allowed to go near any of these. From what I had seen of them, it looked as though they had been partly blown up. I began to wonder whether those remarkably efficient motors had a tendency to explode.

At last the time arrived for me to start out. Never was a man more anxious to begin a compulsory task.

With a chill at my heart, I noticed that Issa was not among those who marched in as we marched out that day. I had known she would not be. When my instructor, in the usual surly frame of mind in which he started his days, entered the car and grunted at me to start, I told him of my fears. He seemed more interested than I had feared he would be.

"I know who you mean, monkey," he said, telling me Issa's number and the number of her car and of her trainer. "Do as I tell you."

He gave his orders more sharply than usual that morning, as though he were excited, and peered intently out through the little telescope in our roof. We followed an unusual route.

"Found them," he barked suddenly. "Left! No, not so much. Just a shade to the left now. Now give her the gun!"

We raced. A distant sound came to my ears, *"Phut!"* Then again, *"Phut, phut!"* They were the sounds of explosions.

"I thought so, monkey," exclaimed my trainer; "it's your mate! Take this!" He handed me a gun similar to the one I had carried as a hunter of Graypec, but smaller and somehow much more efficient and deadly looking. My heart thumped madly, and I peered anxiously ahead.

CHAPTER THIRTEEN

WITH ALL THE SPEED I COULD GET, BUMPING VIOLENTLY, THE sand-car raced towards the distant battle. Although I could still hear the sharp sounds that I knew to be caused by the bursting of the tiny but very destructive bullets from pistols like the one I was gripping so tightly, I could see nothing of the struggle. It was a puff of sand from an exploding pellet that first directed my eyes to the over-turned sand-car, like a beetle lying on its back.

Behind me I heard a fizz like a burning match dropped into water, and knew that my trainer was shooting; but I was too busy looking anxiously for Issa to hunt for possible targets beyond her wrecked car.

Apparently a shot had struck the car near the rear axle, causing it to turn over. Nearby I saw, with an unpleasant shock, the female overseer lying dead; and no wonder, for the explosion had occurred almost under her feet. A moment later I realized that Issa must be alive, for somebody had been putting up a fight, and as there were only two persons in the car, then it must have been Issa.

She must have escaped, for there was now no sign of her. Shots were bursting around us, one blowing away part of our left side. Wildly searching, I saw Issa hiding behind the overturned car. Her chain had been just long enough to enable her to crawl through the bottom of the vehicle.

Beyond her, I saw something move on the edge of a ridge of sand, and I had fired almost before I knew I was doing so. Either it was a lucky shot, or tennis had made

my eye very true, for a tiny, dark brown figure jumped to
its feet at once and fell awkwardly.

Swinging the car in a semi-circle, I halted it beside the
wreck. Issa leaned against the caterpillar track, still chained
by her ankle through the bottom of the car. Blood stained
the sand.

"Onward," directed the overseer.

"The woman is wounded. Let me go to her."

"And have your head blown off. Make sure there are
no more of those fellows first."

There was wisdom in his words, and his gun was aimed
at me from behind. With a sigh, I left Issa, and ran the car
forward. We found the enemy car, similar to our own but
of a rounder shape, which had been stopped by a shot in
the engine. Inside were two dead men, and two more lay
on the sand—four in all.

"Good work," muttered the trainer. "This is the car
that got through the lines and has killed so many recruits
and instructors in the last six months."

"Their food locker is empty," I remarked, for I could
see into it from where I sat.

"I do not suppose they have eaten for weeks, any of
them," he returned. "They could get fresh supplies only by
capturing a car in full war equipment, and we took care to
send only recruits where they were. Bound to get them in
the end."

As he spoke, we turned and headed back. Not eaten for
weeks! I felt sorry for my enemies, one of whom I had
slain. How bitter this long-drawn-out war must be—
helpless slaves on one side, and men faced with
extermination on the other! For the first time I had seen
Gorlemites, whom I had heard of so often. They were
very small men, barely five foot tall and very thin. They

wore singlets, shorts and sandals of dark brown, their prominent noses were thin and hooked, like the beak of a parrot, their jaws were square and lips compressed, and their eyes shone with such determined energy that one almost expected the dead men to spring to their feet and attack one with their bare hands. Thus might the warriors of Attila the Hun, or the Norse Vikings have looked, after prolonged starvation.

It was unnecessary to waste more than a single glance on the female overseer, but my trainer got out to examine Issa, who had apparently collapsed now that the danger was over.

"Well?" I asked, as he got in again.

"The woman is fatally injured. We can do nothing to help her. Leave her and go on."

"Let me see for myself," I barked.

"Waste of time. Go on!"

It was not likely that I would take his word for that, especially as I still held my gun in my hand. He was not expecting any hostile move from me, and when he found himself covered, the astonishment on his face was almost amusing.

"Your punishment for this revolt will be terrible," he growled.

"Put down the gun in your hand," I ordered. "Unhook your whip and throw that down also."

He did not move. Such was his surprise and fury that he seemed about to raise his own gun and shoot; if he had done so, we would have died together.

"I'll give you three seconds," I said, coldly. On the count of three, he obeyed, dropping his gun.

"Don't imagine," he said, "that you can kill me and say that the Gorlemites did it. They'll examine your brain and discover the truth."

But I was not thinking of the future. I was concerned with the wounded woman outside and with nothing else. At my order, he unlocked the chain that held me, and we went outside.

Issa was in a bad way.

"You see," he explained, as though trying to humor me, "how the blood spurts from the wound in her thigh. She is bleeding to death."

I did not answer. I was trying to remember instructions I had received in first aid a long time ago. Slowly, my memory returned. So much bleeding could only mean a severed artery. I searched above the wound until I felt the throb of the artery. Holding it with one hand, I ordered the instructor to remove Issa's chain. I wrapped it tightly around her leg so that it pressed against the artery and stopped the bleeding. Then, making him walk ahead of me, I carried her into the car.

"What strange being are you?" asked my trainer. "No other caveman could have done that." He reached for the liquor cupboard.

"Stand away from there," I ordered him sharply.

He turned back to me in sudden fury. "What's that you say?" he shouted.

"You spoke," I said, holding the gun pointed steadily at him, "of reporting me and having me punished. I shall not let you drink until you have promised to keep silent. Also I have some questions to ask you."

"You think to dictate to me?" he asked in amazement. "You, a savage from Graypec?"

"As you have already said, I am no ordinary savage. I am waiting for your promise." I knew his word was hardly likely to be dependable, but I had to rely on it unless I chose to kill him and try to escape through the desert. Issa and I could hardly expect to live alone in the desert, without food or water. Then, too, Issa needed medical care, so the only thing was to work out a compromise that would permit us to return without being punished.

"If you're going to wait until I promise that," he declared, "you're going to have a long wait. No caveman is going to get the best of me." He folded his arms and stared sullenly at me. As a matter of fact, I was glad to see him adopt this attitude. If he had promised readily, it would have had no value—this way, once he promised, he might keep his word.

Hours passed, but I was in no hurry and the rest would do Issa good. Riding across the rough desert might have made the bleeding worse. Meanwhile, inside the car, without motion to ventilate it, it became as hot as an oven. My own thirst was almost unbearable, so the trainer's must have been far worse since his body was not as hardened as mine. Taking a flask from the cupboard, I drew the cork and held the bottle under his nose. When he snatched at it, I emptied the contents on the floor in front of him.

"Enough," he gasped. "I promise. Let me drink."

I refilled the flask and he emptied it almost at a gulp. "Now, tell me," I said, "why you were so sure that I would never see my mate again."

"Tomorrow she is to go with a party that is leaving for a distant part of the desert to fight," he said. His attitude was almost friendly again. "Her training is finished."

Issa's eyes were open now and she too was listening to him, fear tightening her face.

"And that party?" I asked. "Tell me what I want to know and you can drink all you want to. Give me the details."

"There will be two females and two males with one of us in charge. They start in one of these cars early tomorrow."

"What time?"

"When the group has finished its rest period."

"Why won't I be one of the party?" I demanded. "I am the woman's mate. Surely, where she goes they will take me."

"The party is already chosen. Besides, it's against the law for soldiers to have mates. We find that they are more efficient without, so we always part them. That's why you two were put in different training groups."

It was a harsh law, but knowing as I did the cruel ways of Kilsona and the carefree manner in which sexual relationships were made and abandoned, I was not too surprised.

"If we remained here longer," I said, "wouldn't it be too late for Issa to join this party?"

He shrugged. "It would, but then she would join another in a few days. And you would know nothing about it until she was gone."

"We will return now, then," I said. "You will drive and we will return in a regular manner. But I shall conceal a gun in my mouth in case you forget your promise."

Happier now, having had all he wanted to drink, he answered carelessly: "Do you think I wouldn't keep my promise? I'd be a bigger fool than you are, monkey, to admit letting you get the better of me. If they knew that, they'd say I was incapable of doing my job here and they'd ship me off to the wars. But you'd better watch your step, monkey."

Before we started off, he insisted on cutting off the heads of the four dead Gorlemites and putting them in an airtight locker at the back of the car. This grisly act was done because of the value of heads to him. He would take the credit for the killings and was entitled to two weeks off duty for each head he brought in.

Under his hands, the car raced back toward the base. Issa, still very weak, nestled in my arms. She clung to me and wept bitterly, too miserable to speak at first. Later, she found her tongue and told me that she loved me, even though I was a caveman, because I was kinder to her than anyone had ever been.

The sand-car whirled around and stopped. We were back in the settlement, about three hours before our usual time, with a jagged hole in the side of the car to explain. Stepping past us, the trainer picked up his whip and gun and stalked importantly out.

"Come out, both of you," he ordered.

We alighted, Issa still in my arms. As we made our way to the rest-sheds, I heard the trainer explaining to a group of his fellows how he had shot the four Gorlemites and saved the life of a female slave.

Issa's leg had stopped bleeding, and I told her to lie down in her usual place. So far as I could see, the full gang was there, so that no car could have started off into the desert.

I was beginning to feel how hopeless our position was. There had been a vague idea in my mind of knocking one of the two chosen men unconscious, and taking his place. But how was I to know who had been chosen, or to cut the chain that bound each slave to a post? If I could have done this, I would not have hesitated. As it was, all I could do was slink into a dark corner and wait to see what happened.

Time passed slowly, but I waited as patiently as I had often waited for game in Graypec. The low buzzing of the engine of a sand-car aroused me after a long while. Peering through a crack in the wall, I saw a car halt in the yard between the plank huts. It was obviously a visiting car, its color being much darker than the sand surrounding our settlement. A stout, coarse-looking man got out and was met by two overseers who treated him as though he carried authority. Then my own trainer joined them and seemed to be telling the stranger about our little affair with the Gorlemites. I gathered that the newcomer was showing impatience and asking a lot of questions. Then the four of them began walking toward the hut in which I sat. Quickly, I slipped back into my dark corner.

They entered, one carrying a torch, and bent over Issa. From their low words, I gathered that Issa's wound was not thought serious enough to prevent her traveling. Then the stranger looked on with a dissatisfied air, while the others began arousing the other three. Chains were unlocked and meat and water placed before each chosen slave. There was to be a man and woman of the cave people and a man and woman of the yellow-haired people. Meanwhile, I was creeping foot by foot along in the gloom behind the sleeping figures.

The first awakened slave I reached proved to be the cave woman, so I had to continue. There was more danger of the sharp ears of my fellow slaves being disturbed than there was of the overseers noticing me. Finally, I reached the caveman, who was sitting up and had nearly finished his food. Then began the most difficult part of my plan, for I had to creep close to him without his hearing me, then dispose of him and take his place without making a sound.

Softly, I crept up. His head raised as though he heard me and I lunged forward, choking his cry with an arm around his throat.

"Be still," I whispered, "and you will not be harmed." Feeling my gun against his flesh, he cringed in fear. He could not tell whether a slave or a guard had seized him, but the presence of the gun undoubtedly made him think I was a guard.

"Listen," I whispered, "it has been decided that you are not going to the wars yet. You will stay here and train a while longer. Lie down and keep your eyes closed. If you open them before you are aroused for training, you will be shot. Hear me?" I released his throat, but was ready to clamp down again if he tried to shout.

"Yes, master," he gasped and did as he was told. So implicit was his obedience to his rulers that he did not attempt to look at me.

"Come!" called an imperative voice. I had been just in time. Three other figures rose and shuffled forward, Issa limping badly. I slouched along behind them, my head down, gun hidden in my hand.

Passing through the opening, we went out into the light I feared. I heard Issa whisper, "Goodbye, my darling," and I had to resist an impulse to let her know I was right behind her.

Too late, I noticed that one of the overseers stood just outside the door, checking us. He passed Issa along without a glance, but the next he caught by the hair and turned his face upward.

Although I tried to shuffle quickly past him, he caught hold of me and tilted my face up to the light.

"What is this?" he exclaimed. "This is the wrong monkey."

Other overseers came bustling up. The visitor glared angrily. "Are you sure?" he demanded.

The overseer nodded.

"But how did it happen?" the visitor wanted to know. "Disgustingly careless of you, delaying me this way. Apeman, how did you get here?"

"They woke me, called me out," I mumbled, trying to look abject. It was a good thing the gun was in my hand instead of my mouth, or I might have been caught when I had to speak.

"Fools," snapped the visitor. "You picked the wrong one. I shall report you as unfitted for the soft life here and recommend that you be sent to the desert." He took note of the tabs hanging around their necks and turned back to me. "How long have you been training, monkey?"

"Fourteen days, master," I said.

"Ah, get in, curse you! One cave-animal is as good as another. I've no time to rectify the blunders of fools."

He kicked me and I crawled in joyfully. A minute later, I was at the wheel, following the direction marked out by the long minute hand on the guiding clock-face, while the guard sat at the back and Issa and the other two slaves sat behind me, fear and wonder in their eyes. Each of the stations maintained in the desert by the Larbies had a transmitter similar to but smaller than the blue globe that pulsed over the main station at the mountain; the instruments in the cars were tuned in on the home transmitter and the long hand would remain pointing to that station, making it impossible to get lost.

"Kastrove!" I heard a soft voice say, hushed in surprise. "Quiet, darling," I answered for I was afraid the guard might guess the trick I had played.

Now I began to feel the reaction after the exciting time I had been through and I drove in a semi-doze. I had had no rest, as the others had, neither had I had food or drink. Despite all my efforts, the view ahead would dissolve into a blurry haze—my eyes would dim and my head droop. As a result of my drowsiness, there was a sudden lurch that nearly upset the car and earned me a cursing. I was ordered out of the driving seat and the other male slave took my place.

Then for a long while I slept fitfully, being half aroused by the sharp jolts.

CHAPTER FOURTEEN

MY SLUMBERS WERE ENDED BY A SHARP KICK. THE CAR WAS not moving and it was already night, the desert being utterly black except for a few stars. In the ceiling of the car there was a dim light, shaded so that it could not be seen from outside through the lookout holes. By its pale radiance, I could see that Issa was asleep.

"We are now," said the guard who had delivered the kick, "through the lines and from here on there is danger. At any moment we may meet one of the cars belonging to the enemy; they may even be waiting in ambush for us. From here on there must always be one of you on the lookout, in addition to the driver. That means, seeing one of you is injured, six hours sleep and twelve hours on guard for each one. Now and for the rest of your time in the Desert of Gorlem, your lives will depend on how alert you are. If we fail to see an enemy car before we are ourselves seen, we may all be blown to pieces.

"You will know an enemy car because it will be rounder than one of ours. Directly you see such a vehicle, press the emergency button beside you and our car will stop. Remember that a stationary object is always harder to see than a moving one and when one of these cars stop the effect is often as though it had vanished into thin air. So mark the spot and draw my attention at once. I am giving each of you a gun, but do not use it unless I tell you to."

As I took the weapon, I felt elated by the possession of two guns. I took my turn at watching while the cave-woman drove, then I drove again while the other man looked out. At first, there were many stops as whoever was on duty thought he saw an enemy car, but these delays became fewer as we calmed down enough to distinguish between a car and a shadow.

I drove over a flat tableland of tumbled rocks, then along a rocky valley littered with boulders that were hard to avoid. As daylight began to filter over the desert, the air was so clear and so void of life, vegetable or animal, were the bare black rocks that I almost imagined myself driving over the barren landscape of the moon or some other world from which all life is gone and death is finally, utterly victorious. The Desert of Gorlem was not all sand, about half of it being mountainous or rocky, much like the Sahara.

Among the black rocks, of course, the car showed up more and all of us had to keep a sharp lookout. Anxiously, we watched our detectorphone, which, we were told, would warn us of approaching engines. It was a great relief when we rolled out into the undulating plain again, where one could see for great distances and feel safe from surprise.

The hours passed in dull monotony, driving, looking out over the dreary desert, sleeping briefly with visions of flowing sand before one's eyes, hot shriveling days and cold starlit nights. At times, we passed pulsing blue lights that were minor copies of the big one set on the volcanic mountain and then we could relax our vigilance for a time for no enemy dared to approach these.

Once our guide cursed vehemently when he looked for one of these globes, but failed to find it. As we passed the site at great speed, I caught a glimpse of many sand-cars around a pile of wreckage.

"The fools," our guard said, "failed to keep a proper lookout and got smashed in a surprise attack. Shows what will happen to you if you don't keep your eyes open."

The incident must have affected his nerves, for after that he kept us traveling over the desert at top speed. The ground was firm and level so that a great speed could be maintained hour after hour. At the pace we traveled, it was impossible to keep an efficient lookout; once we were fired at but the enemy could not get up speed quickly enough to follow us. The Gorlemites never avoided battle—they were such fanatical fighters that it was seldom that the sighting of an enemy car ended in any way other than the annihilation of one side or the other.

Our food was compressed and frozen meat, which we took out of our vacuum-lined safe during the early morning hours and ate when it had thawed. Occasionally, we halted at a station under a blue globe to replenish our water supply. Then we would have a brief rest, getting out to walk around.

During one of these halts, at the first light we saw after passing the wrecked station, I heard our guard talking to a man who wore the simple uniform of a station commander.

"The light is out at 743," our guard said.

"Yes," replied the station commander. "They captured the place somehow and you can guess what happened. The light continued by itself for several days and nearly every car attached to the station came in as usual and was captured. Just ran blindly into a trap. Less than a dozen survivors out of two hundred and fifty."

"What has happened now?"

"Well, I've sent for the dreadnoughts as a matter of routine, but you can guess what they'll find—machinery useless, water poisoned, and not a Gorlemite to be seen."

Our guard nodded in gloomy agreement. "Those that were guarding it," he said, "got their reward for being careless."

"Oh, I don't know," the station commander said. He slashed at a flowering weed with the butt of his whip. "I don't know that they *were* careless."

They were taking no notice of me as I stood, pretending not to listen, a few yards away. Still pretending an interest in the other slaves, I sidled a few feet closer.

Our guard was surprised and demanded to know how the station could have fallen except through carelessness. He emphasized that the stations were practically impregnable if they were properly manned. He expressed the fear, a strong note of questioning in his voice, that the Gorlemites must have invented a new weapon.

The station commander seemed to be enjoying the mystery he had created. "No," he said, "nothing new, except perhaps in method. You see—it's the *second generation.*"

"Second generation?" Obviously the remark meant no more to our guard than it did to me.

"Yes, the second generation." The commander looked superior. "These Gorlemites are damned clever. They are always thinking up new schemes. We intend, I think, to underestimate them. We know that they do not have the scientific resources or appliances that we have, but we forget the advantage of their sheer natural cunning, which has become sharpened by despair. The methods which served us well two years ago are no good today."

"But how does this affect 743?" our guard asked.

"We all know," the commander said, his manner clearly indicating that he was going to make the most of being able to propound a theory, "that our slaves are under mental control, that as long as they live they must strive for the cause, that *nothing* can ever make them reveal any of our secrets in any way. But what of the second generation? I know, although no one else pays any attention to it, that the Gorlemites are taking prisoners—especially women. I have checked the number of warriors I have lost in the past three years with the number of bodies found and there is a difference of more than thirty. Only six of these were males."

"But what would this accomplish?" our puzzled guard asked.

"They breed them. The Gorlemites can get no information from a captured slave because they remain under control as long as they live. But mothers will tell their children things, feel a need to pass on information, in fact, and the Gorlemites could then learn anything from the children. The second generation is not controlled."

"But how would that help? What do the slaves know?"

"Enough," the commander said. "They know what our cars are like, the location of stations, the layout of buildings, vulnerable points..."

"But even then—"

"Listen further. What is to prevent the second generation, those children of Gorlemites and slave mothers, from becoming part of the Gorlemite army? Imagine it—a dozen cars, all copied after ours, arrive one after another at one of our stations. From each one, a slave or two get out and wander about. No one thinks anything of this. They look like our slaves, not like Gorlemites. Then at a signal, they attack—from inside the station."

"But—but," stammered our guard, "how is one to know friend from foe? These Gorlemites—they are worse than savages, they know no rules of war."

"Bah! We must face facts, my friend. Why should they fight this war by rules? You and I look forward to lives of ease as chiefs of cave villages or as rulers of parts of the crystal cities after five years here; but for the Gorlemites or our slaves there is no escape from the desert. Naturally, you and I would like this war to be nicely conducted in order that we have greater safety. All we are concerned with—just between ourselves—is living out the five years and getting away from here. But the Gorlemites are concerned with *winning* the war. Naturally, they fight differently than we want them to."

"I suppose so..."

"Now," continued the commander, "where I think we are wrong is this: we are implacable where we should be cunning. *We* must also take prisoners."

At this point, he suddenly noticed me and angrily demanded to know what I was doing there. I fled.

A few hours later, we were again passing through the feathery palms on the outskirts of the station and entering the desert once more. For days, our course lay along the side of a belt of vegetation that marked the course of an underground river. It was strange, after so much desolation, to see many wild animals as we drove along. Stations were also more numerous, owing to the greater water supply and to the need to protect the more desirable sections of the desert.

At last, we arrived at the station that was our destination. It was situated on the edge of what had once been a lake but was no longer more than a bed of hardened clay several miles across. The ground glistened with crystals of salt, but abundant fresh water was always available from the wells.

CHAPTER FIFTEEN

WHEN I FIRST SAW THE STATION, I WAS STRUCK BY SOMETHING oddly familiar about the crude huts, but it was several days before I could find the reason. It says much for the speed with which I was forgetting the days when I was Learoy Spofforth that it took me so long to remember. The huts and the tall central building bearing the blue light were all built of red bricks. In other places, the huts had always been fashioned of rough timber, but here was a building that reminded me of my own world. It stirred up a tremendous longing in me, but it wasn't long before it subsided again. There was little place in the life of a slave for nostalgia of any kind.

Discipline was laxer in this station than in the training quarters and we were permitted a measure of freedom. We were told that the first few days we would be given additional training, but except for the instruction periods we were permitted to wander around the station so long as we did not try to enter certain buildings.

It was after about seven days that I performed, simply because I hated to see a fellow creature in agony, the trivial act which was to have such far-reaching results. But certainly, at the time, I had no suspicion of anything but a simple reaction.

I was prowling through the settlement, utterly bored with everything. The vast, undulating expanse of ochre desert, with its mirages, its sand storms, its creeping dunes that smoked in the winds, its hazy horizon, seemed an everlasting prison for me. All I could look forward to was eventually being killed by an enemy that existed in name only. There seemed no purpose in anything. And I had long ago given up any hope of being restored to my own world. I had seen for myself how difficult it had been for my brother to even locate a planet in this tiny universe of atoms. To have believed that he could eventually locate me, pick me out from hundreds of others who looked exactly like me, would have been the height of folly.

Suddenly, there came to my ears, like an echo of my own misery, a low moan. At first, I thought perhaps it had come from my own lips, an involuntary cry of despair. But when it came again, I knew I was wrong. It was like a cry wrung by unspeakable torture from lips that had been determined to pay no tribute to pain. All the pain in the world seemed to be in that feeble moan.

It stirred me out of my selfish preoccupation with the realization that somewhere near there was another person whose agonies were greater than my own imagined suffering. I listened more closely for the next shuddering gasp and when it came I was able to locate the source.

It came from the other side of the fence that separated the homes of the slaves from the other buildings of the settlement. This fence was a series of sheets of a dark brown metal, fifteen feet high and with an edge like a knife. There was no possible way of getting over it in daylight without being seen, but I thought I might manage it after dark.

When the sun went down that evening, it left behind it a half moon that gave an uncertain light. It would be enough to help me find my way, yet would also make it easier to conceal myself if necessary. It was, of course, against orders to pass any fence without permission, but I was determined to find the person whose suffering I had overheard.

I was sure that I could jump the fence, having jumped as high many times back in Graypec. The muscles of the caveman body I had inherited had been formed for just such leaps. Accordingly, I tied my two guns around my waist, and approached a part of the fence that was in the shadow of several palm trees. I took a short run and leaped with all my strength. There was a slight pain in one knee as it grazed the very top of the fence, then I was dropping softly on the other side.

I crouched there, waiting for several minutes. But there was no sound of alarm and I slipped in among the shadowy bungalows. I had a rough idea of the spot where I had heard the sounds.

Prowling in that direction, I came on a door bolted on the outside. I knew that this could only mean the necessity of keeping something or somebody inside. Softly, I drew the bolt and slipped through the door, closing it behind me. Taking a chance, I felt along the side of the door until

I found the switch. The next instant the place was filled with light.

There was a bloodstained table fitted with machinery, which looked as if it were meant for torture. There were bands obviously meant to fit around ankles and wrists; there was a wheel with numerous blades of sharp, stained steel...

On the concrete floor in front of the table lay the victim of these preparations. He was a Gorlemite—I knew that because he was so small, a dried-up specimen of man. A short brass chain around his neck prevented him from standing up.

There is no need to describe his injuries, but until he opened his eyes I did not think that one so horribly cut could possibly be alive. But when he showed signs of life, I quickly grabbed up the water jug which was out of his reach and offered it to him. He raised a withered arm and tried to push the jug away.

"Tempt me not with water," he whispered in a cracked voice. "I must die."

I whispered that I had come to help him and offered the jug again. For the first time, he turned his dark eyes to my face.

"If you would help me," he whispered, "then kill me. I have asked many times for death, but it is always withheld. You cannot fool me with offers of help. I will reveal nothing about my people. I have willed to die and die I shall."

Somehow, his speech made me realize how futile my gesture of help was. I was a slave, incapable of helping myself, and the most I could offer this Gorlemite was to prolong his life so that the Larbies could torture him further. On a sudden impulse, I placed one of my two guns in his hand and slipped quickly out of the building. He had been right. Death was the only offer that could have any meaning in this place.

Halfway to the fence, I heard the sound of the gun and thought that at last he had his wish. I hurried toward the fence as I became aware that there were dim figures rushing from the other buildings. It wouldn't do for me to be caught.

Back of me, the gun roared again. Then a third time. There were howls of anger from the building. I stopped in amazement. Apparently, the Gorlemite had been more filled with fight and desire to live than I had realized. The first shot must have been him blowing away the chain that bound him, the latter shots had been directed toward the guards.

Not ten feet from where I stood, a guard peered around the edge of a building and fired. There was an answering shot from in back of me and the guard fell dead. Before I could more than grasp the fact, the Gorlemite came racing toward me. I saw the light glint on the weapon in his hand, then he must have recognized me for it shifted. He changed his course and came up to me.

"If you *are* my friend, help me," he said. He fired to the right and I saw another guard drop in the moonlight.

I had little choice. I had already either helped him too much or too little. The sudden turn of events linked my fate with his. My only chance of survival lay in both of us escaping from the station. I motioned him to follow me and headed for the fence.

Knowing that he would never be able to jump the fence, I brought my own gun up and fired at it as we approached. I knew that those explosive bullets would tear huge hunks from steel, but to my amazement the fence was unmarred after I fired. I stopped short.

"The fence—" I gasped. "My shot didn't even scratch it."

"Naturally not," the Gorlemite said. "It's diamond. But you should be able to jump it. Throw me over and then follow yourself."

I was in a panic now for lights were coming on all over the settlement. Quickly, I took him by the ankle and wrist and flung him over the fence. The next instant I followed, with a standing leap that called on every bit of power in the caveman's body. For once I was thankful for the body I had inherited. As I cleared the fence, I heard a shout from behind me—a shout that made it all too clear that my future course was away from the settlement.

"It's Kastrove," one of the guards bellowed.

But with the fence between us and the guards, everything seemed almost peaceful again. We could still hear the shouting, but nobody was waiting for us and we slipped hastily away between the brick barns.

Running and dodging in the dark, we came upon an empty sand-car and a minute later we were inside and racing across the cracked clay of the dried lake. Pursuit had already started, but my reckless driving and the shooting of my companion soon shook them off.

At last, we were hidden in a sparse copse. I was beginning to feel a sense of triumph at having gotten away. And there was a feeling of excitement at what was ahead. There was no question of returning to the station. I would have to go on with my new friend and join the Gorlemites. I could not help feeling that whatever they represented, it would still be better than the Larbies. At least, they were men.

I did have a moment of sorrow at the thought of having left Issa behind, but even that soon vanished under the need to make our escape secure.

Under the guidance of my companion, I went on through the pale moonlight. Both of us wrapped ourselves in the thick cloaks that the car contained for night driving and I settled for a long drive.

"Now," said the Gorlemite, "drive steadily towards the distant mountain peak that can be seen from here in daylight. Within two days time you will come to a rock that the wind and the sand have worn to the shape of a huge, horned lizard about to leap over a precipice. At the foot of the precipice, you will find my people."

With these words, he lay down on the boards to rest, his long fingernails tapping idly on a broad, flat leaf, which he had apparently plucked sometime during our race for freedom. Apparently, he thought it an easy thing to drive a straight line across the desert in the dark, with only an uncertain direction to guide me. Then I realized that the short hand on the indicator in the car was set to point toward the blue globe on the Larbies' main station, I made a mark in relationship to it and was thus able to keep a straight course.

Sunrise found me making my way through a range of dunes. Between these hills of sand, the ground was packed hard by the caterpillar tracks of passing cars. Ascending a low hill, I saw immense dunes stretching away to the west. The low sun, shining among them, gave them many colors, ranging from pink to mauve and changing every minute.

It was a beautiful sight but to have remained there on the hill long would have been dangerous. I hastened on, hoping to find a place where the car would be better hidden. I wanted to stop and look after my companion. I was suddenly remembering his terrible wounds.

I finally stopped the car between two huge dunes and turned to the back of the car. But when I reached the Gorlemite, he was huddled up in a queer attitude. I saw the reason as soon as I bent over him. He was dead and had been for several hours. I remember noticing that the broad leaf was still beneath his hand. I covered him with cloaks and went back to the driving seat.

All that day I made haste towards the distant peaks and during the night I went on by aid of the indicator. There were few supplies in the car and I began to grow hungry and thirsty. When the next morning came, I hid the car and went to sleep.

Sometime that afternoon I awakened, my arms stiff from the steady driving, my throat parched from lack of water. Despite the extra risk, I decided to go on. It wasn't long when, to my delight, I saw the rock that reared skyward like a great horned lizard. Soon after catching sight of this, I stopped for it was getting dark and it wouldn't do to try to creep up on the hideout of the Gorlemites in the darkness.

I was beginning to realize that I was in enough trouble as it was. With my companion dead, there would be no one to vouch for me to the Gorlemites and they would probably treat me merely as another enemy. On the other hand, there was no way of turning back. One of the laws of the Larbies was that no slave might be received in any station other than the one to which he was assigned. And to return to the station to which I was assigned meant only certain death. My only hope was to find some way of making the Gorlemites believe my story.

Accordingly, at the first sign of daylight, I was off again. I drew closer to the landmark without seeing any sign of the Gorlemites, although at any moment I expected them to fire on me.

I came to a level surface that was covered with a layer of fine black dust, crisscrossed with lines where cars had run. Here, I looked back to see a Gorlemite car following me steadily, too far away to be fired upon. Later, others swung in to the right and left of me, keeping pace. I was surrounded, with only one direction to go.

Had my companion still been alive, no doubt he would have told me some way to show my friendly intentions. I caused my engine to make as much noise as possible, hoping that would prove I wasn't trying to hide, and continued on toward the hideout. The Gorlemite cars did not fire at me or try to contact me in any way, but the fact that I was making straight for their settlement showed that I knew where I was going.

For two hours, we kept up our steady advance, the numbers of my escort increasing as we went along. We had just reached the precipice when I heard and felt an explosion beneath the wheels of my car.

At first, I felt fear, but then I realized that it was such a small explosion that it could have only one meaning. They wanted me to stop. I did so and got out, holding up my hands in the gesture of surrender. There was a wait while the surrounding cars drew closer.

So far I had not seen a single person, but suddenly a loud voice boomed from the cliff above me:

"Get out, all of you!"

I shouted that I was alone.

"Be silent, ape-man," the voice said.

Three men suddenly appeared, walking briskly down the slope. I spoke to them but they waved me aside. One of them opened the door at the back of my car and entered. Despite an obvious belief that there might be other cavemen inside, he entered calmly and without hesitation. He found the body at once for I heard him speak sharply to the others, in a language I didn't understand. A moment later he came out of the car.

"There is a mystery here," he said to me, again speaking the language I knew. "How did he die?"

Briefly, I explained the circumstances under which I had helped the dead Gorlemite escape. Then I went on to explain that while I had been a slave of the Larbies, my sympathies were all with the Gorlemites and that I wanted the chance to fight the Larbies. By now the crowd around me had grown to include a dozen or more. They were all small men.

"It may be," said one man when I had finished my story, "that our man was wounded too badly to drive and forced this caveman to do so."

"No," said another, "he has been dead too long. He must have died almost as soon as the journey began."

There was much rapid talk in the language I couldn't understand. I looked from face to face, trying to guess what was going on, but I might as well have been staring at the face of the precipice. At last they reached a decision and one of them produced a length of cord with which my arms were tied tightly behind my back. I had some doubts as to whether it was wise to let them do this, but decided to submit. If I tried to fight, they might well kill me without further discussion.

They began to drag me up the slope of sand, and I was a little uneasy about what they intended to do. Once we were well above the level of the plain, it could be seen that the face of the cliff held many holes, which were so placed as to be hidden from the view of anyone who was on the lower level. Stone staircases came into sight in what I had thought sheer precipice, and up one of these I was made to climb.

We came to a cave where I had to stoop to pass the opening, but a few steps carried me to where I could stand upright. A few yards further and to the left, then a door was closed, shutting out the last trace of daylight.

Someone switched on a light and I found myself in a rocky cavern from which several dark passages ran. The little men were all around me, arguing in their strange language.

In light of later knowledge, I now know what was happening. Among the Gorlemites there were no social castes or rulers who could be picked out by their clothing or by the deference shown them, so that a stranger had no way of knowing a chief or other responsible person. Most of their government was carried on by committees, half of whom would be chosen for their knowledge and half by popular vote. When I arrived, bringing a special problem, there was much difference of opinion as to which was the correct committee to deal with me.

After more arguing, they finally lashed my ankles together so that I was quite helpless. Taking me out into the daylight again, they lowered me down the stone steps with a rope and one of them brought a sort of wheeled truck. On this I was dumped and pushed along a hard path perhaps a half mile from the village.

Raising myself so as to look over the side of the truck, I saw a number of them digging a hole in the sand with spades. It was to be a long hole, just about the right size for a shallow grave.

I had just about given up, when I heard another man running up and shouting something in the strange language. The digging stopped and all of the little men went away, leaving me lying there in the hot sun. Time became a mere numbing of my muscles, an endless burning of the sun into my unprotected eyes, so that I had no awareness of how long I was left there. But suddenly the little men were back, lifting me from the truck and taking the ropes from my hands and feet. I staggered to my feet and drank some water which one of them offered.

I was dimly aware that one of them was explaining they regretted having treated me poorly, but that it was my own fault. Why, he demanded, hadn't I given them the letter?

"Letter?" I asked in amazement.

Then I learned that the broad leaf on which the dead man had been tapping had carried a message. Strange, but the possibility of a written language hadn't occurred to me. I had seen no writing since I had arrived in Kilsona, not even among the Larbies, so I had thought the tapping no more than that. But what my dead friend had written, they told me, had proved that my story was true.

"You were lucky," said one of the little men, "that the leaf was found at all. It was not seen at the time we discovered the body and it was only accidentally that someone found it later on the floor."

CHAPTER SIXTEEN

WITHIN A DAY I WAS WELL AGAIN AND MIXING WITH THE Gorlemites almost as though I were one of them. They answered my questions quite readily, being far less reserved than the other people I had so far met on Kilsona. I was given food and treated quite well. One young man in particular became very friendly and undertook to show me around the village and explain everything to me. I was glad I had left the service of the Larbies for these stem but friendly people.

This village was one of many in the desert, many of them being even larger. The lives of the Gorlemites were almost entirely organized for efficiency in warfare. I learned that there were heavy guns hidden around to protect the village and that in a last resort they had a way of escaping through tunnels in the earth.

Life in the village was very simple, as I had seen it, but I soon learned that the portion of the village I had seen was only half of it. The other half was entirely under ground and it was there that the women and children lived. There, also, the Gorlemites manufactured clothes and weapons. Most of the caves that made up the upper part of the village had tunnels leading to shafts which dropped to the lower levels. There were wire cages in these shafts, in many ways similar to early elevators on my own planet. I began to have visions of a huge series of cities and passages far under the desert, the whole sub-strata of the desert honeycombed with secret caves and tunnels.

No, my friend told me, they were not yet at that stage. But he added that a few of the larger cities were connected by underground passages, although for the majority of the villages the only way of communicating was by using the sand cars. Thus, when the scientists discovered any new weapons, they were dated to come into use a half year afterwards so that the news and blueprints would have time to reach all of the villages.

This was the first that I had heard about the scientists of Gorlem. I wanted to know more about them.

My friend frowned. He was not sure whether he was doing right in revealing such important matters, but he finally decided to tell me some of the facts.

I learned that the capital of Gorlem was the city of Impel, somewhere in the most barren part of the desert. While every village more or less stood on its own feet, so far as they were governed by a central government, they were ruled by Impel. That City was built entirely underground, being a half-mile below the surface. No persons other than scientists or servants of scientists might visit the city except after a long journey in a windowless sand car. My friend had once been there, but he had no idea where it was located. This had been in his youth and he had brought away little more than a dim, awed memory of endless corridors and mighty machines.

"That is where I should be," I lied. "I am a scientist."

"Is it possible?" my friend asked in astonishment. "We'll have to see what the committee says."

Several hours later, I went before the committee in person. The meeting was informal, a group of men crowding around me, all talking at once, asking me questions and discussing my answers. They seemed quite friendly and willing to give me all the help they could without harming the village or breaking the laws.

"We do not understand, Kastrove," one of them said. "How can you, a savage as anyone can see, be a scientist? It is unnatural."

Had they heard, I asked, of transferred personalities?

Long ago the scientists of Kilsona had been able to transfer personalities from one man to another (Issa had told me that) and I had been so treated.

They stared, more puzzled than before, but it happened that two of them had heard these legends of the wonders that men could perform when civilization was at its height on Kilsona. But they wanted to know what proof I had of this.

To prove that I was really not a savage, I offered to work out any mathematical problem they might care to give me. It was well known that the cavemen could not count above ten and I took a chance that these Gorlemites would not know any mathematics too complicated for me. But I didn't have to do that for my friend interrupted to say that the fact I knew about the scientists of old was proof enough.

Then they wanted to know where I came from, if not from Graypec. It was a question I had been expecting, but I still had no answer ready for it. When I had tried to tell Issa where I came from it had only served to convince her that I must be a spy, so I decided not to try that a second time. The truth was much too wild for these simple, practical people. So I tried something else on the spur of the moment.

"Why," I said, trying to sound casual, "haven't you guessed the answer to your own question? I am one of your own race from the city of Impel. A group of us discovered the lost secret and I went forth as a spy in the ranks of the enemy."

It was, I thought, quite a good invention for the time being. I saw that they were looking at one another, astonished, but impressed. If they believed me, they must send me to Impel and perhaps when I got there the scientists would believe my real story—perhaps even be able to find some way of restoring me to my own body and world. But that was too much to hope for and I pushed the thought from my mind.

"Yet you do not understand our speech," objected one member of the committee.

"Oh, that!" I said, thinking fast. "The process I went through caused me to forget that and many other things. But all my memories will be restored when I am restored to my own body in Impel."

"If you are indeed of Impel," the chairman of the committee said, "we must return you there. But why didn't you tell us before?"

"I didn't want to rush back to a life of safety and ease," I said, trying to appeal to feelings they understood. "I wanted a chance to live the life of a warrior in the sunlight."

"And you found," said the chairman, "that you had overestimated your abilities and that it is not easy to be a soldier." Several men smiled at his words and I felt easier. "Whether or not the story we have heard is true, we cannot say, although it seems to be reasonable and seems to agree with the few facts we know. The only men who can say whether it is true or not are the men of Impel themselves. I think it is our duty to send Kastrove there at once."

He was using his power as chairman to end the discussion and there were some who seemed to want to ask me more questions, but in the end the committee agreed. I was to be taken to the secret city of Impel. Until I got there, I would be out of danger.

"You are pleased at the findings of the committee, I suppose," my friend said when we were together again.

"Yes, thanks to you. But it was a close shave, wasn't it?"

"More so than you think," he said. Then he added casually: "They are hard to deceive, but between us we did it."

I realized, with a shock, that he did not believe my story at all.

"I don't know," he continued, "who you really are, or where you come from, Kastrove, but you will have to tell a better tale than that when you get to Impel. I understand that our scientists can ferret the truth out of the most unwilling brain."

Bewildered, I faced his grim gaze. "Then you do not believe me?" I asked.

"You wear out my patience, Kastrove," he said. "When you came here you were in danger of death and my brother—for it was my brother you saved and this is why I have helped you—had written a letter to me with the object of saving you. Yet you left it on the floor of the car and said not a word about it even when you knew you were about to be killed. Would you have us believe that you had forgotten that you had a written language, as well as forgetting how to speak your mother's tongue?

"Kastrove, I have repaid you for rescuing my brother. From now on, I do not wish to see you again, for you have caused me to betray the trust reposed in me, by helping you to go to Impel, and I do not wish to be reminded of that fact." With that, he turned and stalked away.

Preparations for my journey were soon made. Once the decision was reached, they were anxious to send me on my way for I consumed too much of their slender reserves of food. By the second day, one of the cars was ready to take me. Three of the Gorlemites were going with me and we would all take turns driving the car.

We left quietly, without ceremony, for there was no one gathered around to say goodbye to us. No doubt my three companions had fathers, brothers and sons, but they showed no feeling about leaving. We started off on our long and dangerous journey with no more fuss than if we were merely taking a short drive around the desert.

Considering the numbers of men and women patrolling the desert, alert to kill, it would seem almost impossible to run across it for many days without running into a battle. But we accomplished it. Save for a few stops for water, we drove steadily and within a few days reached the village of Elboaz, on the edge of the desert within a desert where the scientists of Gorlem lived and where my bluff would be called.

At Elboaz, we rested after our journey and we were examined about the purpose of our trip. We needed the rest badly, but I would have sooner kept on than to have been made to realize that my fateful interview was so close to hand. The important leaders of Elboaz examined us.

"One Kastrove, an ape-man from Graypec, of first generation, to be taken to the town of Impel," muttered the man who scanned my record. "Most unusual thing to do. Irregular too. Doubt if I can arrange it."

It took a long time to persuade him to let me pass. "But what right had your committee—" was his continual refrain.

He gave my companions the latest news and orders to take back—a new process for making explosives, a more powerful and silent type of engine for the cars.

My stay at Elboaz was a very short one. My companions, who had come with me across the desert, could go no farther and I set out again with a small party that happened to be going to the capital. The journey took about twelve hours and I could see nothing of the country we passed through, though we seemed to be steadily climbing most of the time. Part of the time I slept.

When I got out of the car, I did not at first realize that I was underground. It was more like being in some rambling stone building without windows, an impression I never lost while I was at the capital.

Impel was a pleasant surprise, the homes of the scientists being decorated and furnished in a way that was almost luxurious when compared with the other homes I had seen on Kilsona. The scientists of Impel were both men and women, husband and wife usually working together, for they were the only people who practiced marriage as it was known on my world. Each couple had an average of three servants. There were three classes— servants, laboratory helpers, and scientists. Hereditary rights did not exist, but a marriage out of one's class was forbidden. Children were graded according to intelligence when quite small and those of low standards were sent out to the fighting stations. The reverse also took place; in fact, about a third of the population of Impel had been born at fighting stations.

All of this, naturally, I did not learn until later, but on this, my first sight of the underground capital, I did notice that there were chairs on which one could really rest, couches which were comfortable, walls tastefully decorated, and cool fresh air which drifted continually through doors which were seldom closed. For a while, I was made to wait in a room where several clerks worked at desks, entering up records and working out sums by means of complicated calculating machines.

Someone beckoned and I followed through an extensive library. The writing was strange, but I could see by some of the pictures that it was a fairly complete scientific library. I began to have hope. Here, if anywhere on Kilsona, I could expect to be met with understanding.

No notice was taken of my passage. I supposed that the clerks took me for a subject of experimentation.

I soon found myself before a white-haired man with spectacles of strong magnifying power. He was sitting at a desk and peering into a microscope. He waved me into a chair, then nodded to someone behind me. Instinct made me turn around, but it was too late. A firm metal bar snapped across my chest and a second later I felt metal bands snapping around my legs. Unable to move more than my arms and head, I was wheeled into a corner and left. Presently, two other men joined the white-haired man and they came over to me. They wheeled my chair away from the wall so they could stand around me. I could partly follow their talk by the reason of them prodding, from time to time, the part of me about which they were talking. They used long pointers for this so as to keep out of the range of my arms. I sat as patiently under this treatment as I could.

"You're behaving very well, Kastrove," one of them said in the language I knew. "Cavemen we have here for study usually struggle and bellow—kick up no end of trouble."

"I am not an ape-man," I replied, trying not to let my irritation show. "I know that my story is so strange it is difficult to believe, but give me a chance and I can prove it."

At that they laughed.

"You know," said one of them, "that you should never have been allowed in here. The chief of Elboaz says that you made a silly claim of being a transferred personality and he thought that you might prove an interesting mental study. It is absurd. Why should we be interested in an ape-man's mind?"

"I think I see the chief's point," one of the others said.

"The mere fact of an ape-man knowing *anything* about transference is unusual in a way. How did you know about it, Kastrove?"

"Because I am a transferred personality," I replied.

"Now, see here, Kastrove," the scientist said, "if you'd made that claim, say, ten thousand years ago, it might have been believed, but the secret has now been lost that long. So far as I know, no one is even trying to find the secret. It could only be done if you combined it with time travel, sending your disembodied spirit into the future or the past. Is that how you did it, Kastrove?"

I was determined to tell these men nothing but the truth and so I shook my head.

"I see," he said. "Then your fairy tale does not include anything so wild as that. Then where *do* you come from?"

"This whole world of Kilsona," I said, "circling its sun, is but a part of an atom in a larger universe—and I am from that universe."

There was a moment of stunned silence, then the white-haired man said: "Now, that is plainly impossible because—"

"Shut up," another scientist snapped. He turned to me. "I suppose an atom on your scale is very similar to ours. Describe an atom for us."

I knew this was a test question and I thought hastily of all I could remember reading about atoms. I was distinctly sorry that I had not taken a greater interest in science. But I managed to talk for several minutes about protons and electrons, their relative weights and their equal and opposite electrical charges.

"That'll do," the scientist said. "You know something about it but not much. But you are claiming that while you were examining an atom in your universe, you found us on an electron? Is that it?"

"Not on an electron. In the atom, we discovered a whole system of planets—probably formed from a broken proton, independent of the electrical scheme of the atom." I was glad to remember a phrase from my brother's explanation.

"That will do. You are certainly no ape-man. But if you are a transferred personality, then you must be a Larby."

They pushed me back into the corner and left the room without giving me another glance. I was left to spend the night strapped in the chair without food or drink. Early the next morning, the white-haired scientist again entered the room.

"Taking a balance of the chances," he said, "we think you might be a Larby. But even so, being a transferred personality, you will make an interesting study. Now our methods of study depend on your cooperation, but you can rest assured that it will not be long before we know the truth about you. First, let me ask you a few questions."

He went on to cross-examine me as to the earth I came from, its people, its vegetation, its animal life. I answered in some detail.

"Queer," he said at last. "In spite of the strangeness of the things you describe, you more than half convince me. It's too fantastic a tale for even a Larby to dream up. To think that you might be some sort of being who, by flicking dust from your sleeve, hurls into space millions of worlds like Kilsona. It's impossible."

"Millions of suns," I corrected him. "Planets are fairly rare."

"Yet," he continued, ignoring me, "your personal achievements are slight. According to you, the knowledge your people have is less than ours, yet there do seem to be points where you might be able to give us something. I was particularly interested in your reference to ultra-sonics, although you seemed to have few details. You are full of stimulating suggestions that fade into nothing on close examination. It's irritating. How do you come by all this half knowledge?"

"In my youth," I said, "I was made to read many textbooks, but I'm afraid that the knowledge I got from them faded away during the later years."

"So," he murmured, leaning back with half-closed eyes, "you are a storehouse of information that cannot be tapped."

Sinking into a deep reverie, he seemed to forget all about me once more. But he finally stirred and muttered:

"Ever heard of the unconscious mind, Kastrove? No man knows what amazing capacities our brains have for storing information. If an average man could set down on paper everything he has seen and heard, he would fill a library. Even when we have forgotten things, they are only dormant. Many of our mental experts believe that nothing a man has ever seen is ever forgotten, but merely stays filed in the unconscious waiting for the right association to call it forth... Perhaps, if you'll let us try, we can get at the information you've forgotten."

"How?" I asked.

"In the same way that the Larbies turn ape-men into slaves—by hypnotism. That is their only use of it, but we use it in education, medicine, many ways."

I can't say that I altogether liked the idea, but it did seem to be one way of making these scientists recognize the truth. And unless they did, there was little hope for me.

"Very well," I said. "When do we start?"

"As soon as you've had food and drink, I will take you to one of our mental doctors."

Then I had the most enjoyable meal of my life. For one thing, I was almost starving and then it seemed like ages since I had tasted well-cooked food. I always had a good appetite, but I think that on that occasion I broke all records. After such a meal, I felt that I didn't care what happened.

The mental doctor was a woman, a plump cheerful person of about thirty. She greeted me in a friendly fashion, but immediately got to the point.

"In bringing about a state of hypnotic trance," she began, "you must not think that I have to do all the work while you just let me get on with it. On the contrary, you will have to work as hard as I do. To begin with, I want you to concentrate your thoughts on what I am saying, driving out all other thoughts. Gradually, you will find this getting easier…"

She pattered on and I gave my full attention to what she was saying although none of it seemed very important. I had a sense of drifting away, of being very comfortable, and her voice was almost like a gentle music. After a long while, I heard her saying as though from a great distance: "You are to wake up now. You can wake up now. Wake up!"

Opening my eyes, I saw both of the scientists beaming at me with great delight.

"An excellent subject," the woman said. "A perfect deep trance on the first attempt."

"Wonderful," said the other. "Kastrove, you should be proud of yourself. Ah, what wonderful vistas of knowledge will be opened to us. I shall set to work at once to learn your earth language so as to hear it all without making you translate it into the tongue you learned in Graypec."

After that, I spent many hours in a real, refreshing sleep. For the first time, I began to feel at ease. My only worry was about what might be happening to Issa back in the settlement of the Larbies.

I was allotted the home of a servant, but even that was a luxury after the caves on Graypec and the huts of the Larbies. I did no work and they seemed content with the sort of unconscious contribution I was making. Every day, I saw the mental doctor and she would put me into a trance for an hour or so. The white-haired scientist was always there and I understood that he had been assigned to spend all of his time working with me.

After eight days, I was promoted to the rank of a laboratory helper and was given better quarters. I began to put on flesh because in the desert I had become run down to the point of skin and bones.

One thing began to strike me about Impel. As long as I'd been there I had never seen a sick person. I asked the white-haired scientist about this one day.

"We believe in keeping healthy," he said. "From childhood on, we are all carefully watched to see that we get the essential vitamins and that there are no reasons for psychosomatic illnesses to develop. We find that much more is accomplished if everyone also has a healthy mind. There is no reason that a happy person should become ill."

I'm not sure that I accepted this, but it was true that I never did see an ill Gorlemite.

My life was now a strange one, my day's work consisting of lying at ease, going into a trance of some duration, and then coming out of it, my throat dry with talking. Later, they managed to get me to write while in the trance. Then I would awaken to find pages and pages of English writing, setting forth things I had no memory of ever knowing. Often, it was so complex that I couldn't understand what I had written in the trance, but it seemed to be clear to the scientist who worked with me.

Soon there was no need for the woman doctor, as I had learned to go into a deep trance with the use of a simple cue word.

Weeks and months passed and I was promoted to the rank of a first class scientist, which was my first indication that they considered the information that they were receiving was valuable.

"Do you know," the white-haired scientist said to me one day, "you have turned the work of Impel upside down. Nearly everything we were doing before you came has been put aside and our energies are being devoted to working on suggestions that have come from you during your trances."

My first reaction was one of relief because this was proof that my story, fantastic as it was, finally was believed. Then I felt curious, remembering his first impressions.

"But I thought my world was behind yours in knowledge," I said.

"So it is, on the whole. But the field of knowledge is so great that there are many points where your people have found something that we have missed. Some of these points have proved to be mistakes on your part and others lead nowhere, but we still believe that the information we're getting from you will permit us to advance as much in the next two years as we might have normally in the next two generations."

All seemed happy enough, but there came a time when my contentment seemed to grow blurred, like gathering clouds heralding a coming storm. I had a feeling of tension and a fatigue which rest could not banish. The white-haired scientist must have noticed it for one day the mental doctor was in to see me again. She looked into my eyes, asked me a number of questions, and announced that I was suffering from nervous strain and overwork.

"Lucky man," the white-haired scientist said when she announced her decision. "This will mean a good rest for you, with all of the resources of Impel being devoted to nursing you back to health—soft couches, dreamy music, delightful pictures, companionship—"

I made a gesture of impatience. "What is worrying me," I said, "is the thought of my mate, Issa, a woman of Teth--Shorgo, a crystal city in Graypec. She is a slave of the Larbies and I keep wishing I could bring her here."

"I knew it," the doctor cried. "I knew there was some irritating thought in your mind, but I couldn't find what it was and so couldn't remove it. So that's it! Your mate! Well, we'll soon put that right."

"How?" I asked.

"By making you forget," she said.

"No, please," I exclaimed. "I don't want to forget. I have grown very fond of Issa."

"But you would be much happier. We will find another mate for you, instilling in her the thought that you are a fine handsome man so that you will not have to worry about the fact that your appearance is that of an ape-man.

You know, it is not what things are that makes us unhappy, but what we *think* they are."

Despite her conviction, I was not to be persuaded.

"Well," she said, with a shrug, "it is against the law to make suggestions to a citizen of Impel against his will. We can order a servant or laboratory helper to be executed, but we cannot hypnotize one if he doesn't wish to be. What would you like to do, Kastrove?"

By now, I explained, the excitement caused by my dramatic departure from the station of the Larbies would be forgotten. But I still wore around my neck the disc that gave me the right to enter. It might be possible for me to drive a sand-car into the shrubbery near the station and walk into the settlement. Then I could find Issa and bring her away with me.

"Perhaps," the scientist said, "but have you considered the dangers of that long double journey?"

But in the end, I had my way and an escort was arranged for me. I was given a disc bearing the words: *Accepted as a first class scientist of Impel, now engaged on important investigations in which he is to be given every possible help.* This was stamped with the sign of the ruling committee of Impel and thus equipped I set forth once more across the desert.

CHAPTER SEVENTEEN

WITH THE BEST SAND-CAR IMPEL COULD PROVIDE AND SIX crack fighters to guard me on the way, I went out from Impel much more quickly than I had come. Day after day, we raced across the desert, running day and night.

At the Gorlemite village where I had first appeared, a number of warriors met us, for the size and speed of our

car had attracted their attention. They showed great surprise when they recognized that the leader of the car was
the caveman who had left them many months before.
They were sure that I had been on my way to be executed.

Leaving them to talk with my guards, I went into one of
the larger caves and asked about the man who had be-
friended me. He was soon found and was very pleased to
see me, for he had lost his position on the committee as a
result of helping me, but my return as a first class scientist
proved that he was right. He wanted to know if I could
use my influence to get him admitted to Impel as a laboratory helper.

I promised to speak for him when I returned to Impel
and went on to tell him my purpose in returning.

Never had I seen him look so upset. His hands
trembled, his nostrils quivered. He spluttered something
about not believing that I could be serious—that it was
unthinkable for a first class scientist to go alone into an
enemy settlement. He wanted to call a committee together
and discuss plans. Perhaps, he said, they could make an
attack on the enemy station and carry Issa off for me. He
offered to lead the raiding party himself.

"No," I said. "You would be killed to a man, perhaps
before you could even get out of your cars. Besides, Issa
might be killed in the fighting. I will go alone."

After considerable argument, for they seemed to think it
would be their fault if a first class scientist was hurt or
killed, it was agreed that one man would go in a car with
me and another car would escort us until we reached the
settlement of the Larbies. Then my driver would get into
the other car and return and I would be on my own.

Early that night, we started out across the desert. Despite the danger I knew I would have to face, I was elated at the idea of soon seeing Issa again.

It was already dark, two days later, when we first saw the blue light. The two cars stopped back of a sand dune.

"All right," I said to my driver. "You can hop out and get into the other car now."

He grinned. "I'll be all right," he said. "I'll drive you in and wait. Someone will have to look after the car while it is hidden, otherwise you might come out in a hurry and find it gone."

It was a point that hadn't occurred to me and I had to admit it was a good one.

Searchlights from the central tower of the station were soon flashing about the desert, sweeping over the sand like searching fingers. We dodged through them and reaching a patch of shrubbery we hid the car and remained inside waiting for sunrise.

When the sun rose, I got out of the car and pushed my way through the bushes. In the bad light, I had to go carefully to avoid brambles and tripping roots. It was bitterly cold. My identification tab as a Gorlemite was behind me in the car. I wore only my badge of slavery, one of the rough cloaks used by the slaves in the desert night, and leather sandals. My hands were bare.

For about a third of a mile, I ran along in the swinging manner I had learned in Graypec, until I was attracted by the sounds of the chopping of wood and shouting voices. A group of ape-men were collecting fuel for cooking purposes and for the overseers' fires. I quickly joined them and set to work helping to load the wood. Not one of the workers noticed that a stranger had joined them and the fact gave me confidence. In about an hour, we had loaded two trucks and seen them off. We put on our cloaks and walked into the settlement.

Soon I was among the brick barns that served the slaves as houses. I had not been recognized and I was resolved that if anyone should do so I would kill him before he could announce the fact.

The first thing I had to do was to find Issa. The ape-men and the yellow-haired people from the crystal cities occupied different parts of the settlement because they were liable to quarrel if allowed to mix too freely. Too, I'm sure the Larbies realized that lack of contact helped to fan whatever racial antagonism existed.

I thought it likely that Issa, perhaps thinking me dead, for some time had passed since my escape, might have moved back with her own people, so I began my search among the yellow-haired women. I knew that there was a good chance that she had been killed in battle, but this thought I shoved into the back of my mind.

For a while I prowled around, causing many a woman to start in fear when she found an ape-man peering at her intently. It became increasingly hard to dodge the overseers and I was beginning to get desperate. Finally, I stopped one of the yellow-haired men and asked where I could find a woman named Issa, explaining that an overseer had sent me looking for her. He glared at me with suspicion, but finally told me that he had last seen her going toward the outskirts of the station.

By this time, I had been everywhere in the settlement—washing place, sleeping place, cooking place—and I must have been getting careless, for as I made my way toward the edge of the settlement, I suddenly found myself facing a young man I had known at the original training quarters. On seeing me, he looked astonished.

"Why, Kastrove," he exclaimed. "How—"

His words died away as my knife plunged into his throat. I hated to kill him, but I dared take no chances.

Quickly, I looked around to see if there had been any witnesses. I saw no one, but I heard the pounding of feet as someone ran away back of the buildings. I had been seen and soon the overseers would be looking for me and it was possible that the yellow-haired people would also be prowling around looking for revenge. By this time I had figured that Issa was probably working on the small farm that joined the settlement, so I turned and hurried in that direction.

The farm was strongly fenced against thieving animals and had two wells that provided water for the irrigation system. Pushing open a gate and walking in, I found a group of women slaves gathering vegetables in the field. To my delight, Issa was among them.

It was no use rushing straight up to her because she was in the middle of a small crowd and it was against orders for an ape-man to mix with the city people when they were working. I had to arrange to see Issa alone.

I managed to hide myself in some shrubbery without having been spotted by anyone and waited patiently while the work continued.

I had arrived when the morning's work was nearly done and so I knew that I would not have to wait too long. It was perhaps an hour later when the overseer called off the workers and then drove away with the truck. The pickers walked to the nearest well, gulped down water and then went to stretch out in the shade of the small palm trees and shrubbery. It was near noon and they would have an hour or so to rest. Most of the slaves were soon asleep and I moved over to a spot near where Issa was lying.

I tried calling to her softly, but she too was asleep and didn't hear me. Then I threw a small stone, which awakened her. As soon as I saw her eyes open, I called softly: "Issa, Issa!"

"Who is it?" she demanded, looking frightened. She was unable to see me and looked around uncertainly.

"Come over here," I called. "Near the well. I want to talk to you."

Still looking frightened, she came. As soon as she saw me, her face lit up. "Kastrove," she said. She stared at me in amazement and I was conscious of feeling hurt that she did not immediately run into my arms.

"Come and sit beside me," I said. "I want to talk to you."

She moved closer, but still kept a distance between us. "You ran away," she accused me in a dull, lifeless voice. "With an escaped prisoner. You left me and went to the enemy—to your own people, the Gorlemites."

"Let me explain," I said. "Come, Issa."

She came closer, but still not within reach. Not since our first days in Graypec had she been so aloof.

"I always knew you were a spy," she said, "but I shielded you. Why have you come back to expose me to more danger?"

"I came to get you," I said simply. "I can take you where you can be happier than you ever were even in Teth-Shorgo. Listen, Issa—we can slip away through one of the gates now. I have a car and friends waiting. You'll never have to be a slave again."

She wrinkled her brows in the little puzzled frown I knew so well. "I do not understand," she said. "You want me to run away—with you? After all this time?"

"Of course," I said. "I still love you, Issa. I came for you the first chance I had."

"Yes, but—" she began and then stopped. It was as though she had something to explain, but found it difficult.

"What's the matter?" I demanded.

"Don't you see, Kastrove," she said, her voice low. "You went away—left me. I though you were dead—or tired of me. Anyway—"

She stopped again, but this time I guessed it and it was like a blow in the face. "You took another mate," I said.

She nodded. "What else could I do? What did you expect?"

"It matters not," I said after a moment. "You were mine first. You must come with me."

"No. I cannot."

"You must," I insisted. "I'll make you."

"Please talk more quietly," she said, glancing with fear toward the sleeping slaves. "We shall be discovered and you will be killed and I will be punished. Go away, Kastrove, while you can. I will say nothing about it."

A false calm came over me, hiding my mixed emotions. "I'll not go without you," I declared with finality.

One of the slaves stirred and sat up. Issa went quickly back and threw herself to the ground. I slipped back into the shrubbery, determined to wait as long as necessary. I was aware of the sound of shots and shouting from the direction of the village and realized that there must be some rioting as a result of the man I had killed. Such was my mood that I did not care.

It was some time later that a small stone struck me in the side. I looked around to see Issa standing not six feet from me, beckoning. I crawled to her side.

"They know you are here and the guards are looking for you," she whispered. "I had to come to help you escape."

"Then you do still love me," I said. My elation was so great that I thought nothing of the danger. I threw one arm around her shoulders and ran openly toward the gate, pulling her with me. I saw a couple of slaves moving as though to intercept us, but two quick shots from my gun took care of them. An overseer showed up as we neared the fence, but I shot him before he could more than raise the gun in his hand.

Issa was running beside me as we made for the gate. There was no pursuit. Then ahead of us there appeared a lone man, a yellow-haired slave, showing both of his hands, which were empty.

"Don't shoot," Issa cried when she saw him.

Wondering why she said this, I watched the young man as he drew near.

"Not that way, Kastrove," he shouted as he came closer. "Follow me." He turned and ran off at an angle.

I hesitated, wondering if it were a trap, but Issa immediately ran after him. Bewildered, I followed. He led us to one of the trucks nearby, gestured, and the three of us climbed aboard. Immediately the truck shot away, our new friend driving.

We drove through a gate and found ourselves on a sort of tarred road, except that some rubbery material had been used instead of tar to bind together the crushed rock. Along this, we made great speed.

"Anyone following?" the driver shouted.

I glanced back. "Yes," I said. "Two trucks have just appeared."

"They will never catch us," he said. "We have too good a start."

"Where are we going?" I demanded in sudden suspicion. I had noticed that we were heading for one end of the station instead of toward the desert where my car was hidden.

"Trust me, Kastrove, servant of Impel," he answered. He seemed to know all about me.

"Who is he?" I asked Issa, suddenly remembering that she had apparently recognized him.

"My mate," she said.

Then this was the man I had dreamed of murdering after my first talk with Issa. I wondered why he was helping me—or if he were only pretending to help me in order to turn me over to the guards. My hand tightened on my gun.

We were among the scattered bungalows on the edge of the station and not far away there was considerable shooting.

"Where are you taking us, Zimbo?" Issa shouted at the young man.

"Trust me," he said again. He concentrated on driving for several minutes, then braked the truck to a fast stop. "Out," he cried. The three of us jumped to the ground. A moment later, the empty truck started up and raced away toward the desert.

"Our pursuers will follow the tracks until at least one of the trucks gets stuck in the sand," said Zimbo. He turned and knocked on the door of the nearest hut.

The door was opened from the inside and we saw two women inside. Then we were through the door and it was slammed and bolted.

"Who are these?" I heard someone ask.

"Kastrove and Issa," Zimbo said, but he did not complete the introduction by telling us who the others were. A glance at Issa showed me that she was as puzzled as I was. I saw that the single room of the hut had been fitted up almost like a fort. Thick steel plates covered the walls and there were a number of long narrow windows, wider on the inside than on the outside, such as I used to see in the old Norman castles in England. The regular windows were covered with steel shutters. And there was evidently a trap door cut into the floor.

"Splendid," said another man before I could ask any questions. "Now we are all here."

"What do we do now?" asked Zimbo. "Leave these two in safety here and go out and join the fight? Or shall we send them along the tunnel?"

"Neither," the other man said. Apparently he was in charge. "If we went out now, we might even be shot down by our own side. Our duty is to stay here and guard the tunnel. We have done our part in these long dangerous months of spying."

At the last words, Issa let out a sharp cry of surprise.

"Warn that woman to be quiet," the leader said. "And take away her weapons. She is probably still under some hypnotic control." Zimbo stepped over and disarmed her, but no move was made to take my weapon—which was a good thing.

"Who are you and what is happening?" I demanded.

"Tell him, Zimbo," the leader said.

"It's like this," Zimbo said, turning to me with a friendly grin. "Although the committee in our village permitted you to have your way in coming here, because you are a first class scientist of Impel, they felt it necessary to give you protection. We were already here, preparing for the destruction of this station, so we were told to watch for you and to give you aid and to strike at the station the minute you were safe."

"Wait a minute," I said. "You're going too fast for me. First, are you Issa's mate?"

"Yes," he and Issa said together.

"And who else are you?" I demanded of him.

"I," he said proudly, watching Issa's face, "am a soldier of Gorlem and therefore of Impel—at your orders. My parents were from Teth-Shorgo, forced slaves of the Larbies, and my mother bore me after she was captured by the Gorlemites. I was brought up to fight for them, to help destroy the ruthless dictatorship of the Larbies. The same is true of my comrades here."

I remembered the time one of the station commanders had guessed that this was what the Gorlemites were doing.

There was a low moan from Issa. "Then I am a prisoner?" she asked.

"Yes," said Zimbo, "but you need not worry, Issa. Kastrove has plenty of influence to protect you."

"Go on with your story," I said.

"Well, the six of us were established here as spies shortly after you first escaped. Owing to the slack organization, with all of the guards and commanders only interested in themselves, we found it very easy. And all of this time we have been preparing for the battle which is now taking place."

I had been aware for some time that a major battle was raging outside, but now it seemed to be slacking off.

"Yes," said Zimbo, as though he guessed my thoughts from my face, "the battle must be almost over. Our soldiers were waiting out in the desert and a number of others were hidden throughout the village, having entered through this tunnel. Such crossfire quickly wins."

He had thrown open the trapdoor in the floor while speaking. It disclosed a round black hole across which a stout metal bar held a rope. There were pulleys by which a man could pull himself up or lower himself down into the blackness.

"Our secret tunnel," Zimbo said. "We drove it under the clay of the dried lake through the solid rock right to the central building of the station. From beneath that central building, our men released a deadly gas when the fighting started. That is why the battle is almost over so quickly. In another few minutes, we can leave here and go back to our own village."

That served to remind me of my own loss, yet I felt that I must not take my anger out on this man who had helped to save my life. "Well," I said, "what has happened is done. I hope you will be happy, Zimbo, and you, Issa."

He misunderstood me. "I am proud," he declared, "to have been of service to you in looking after Issa for you while you were away." I realized that he and Issa both looked at the matter in this light; it was part of the queer and primitive attitude of all Kilsonans towards sex.

"I would not take her from you," I said dully.

He appeared surprised. "You are my ruler," he said. "If you want my life, it is yours. If you want my woman, she is also yours."

"Then the wishes of the woman must be considered," I said.

He rolled his eyes as though to express the queerness of my suggestion. But he turned to Issa and said: "Choose him. You will be comfortable at Impel."

Issa came to me and put her face on my chest. Her manner was so warm that I knew it was what she wanted and not mere obedience. I put my arms around her, brushing my lips across the yellow hair.

"I'm happy now," I murmured.

"And I," she said. "I loved you always, Kastrove, but I had given my promise to him. Now that he has released me from it, I am happy."

"When we get to Impel," I told her, "you will soon get some flesh over those bony ribs you have now."

And she did.

Back at the capital, I lived happily with Issa. The scientists removed the hypnosis the Larbies had placed on her and there was nothing to mar our life together. I'm sure that my work as a scientist puzzled her as much as it did me, but then that work was soon at an end for they seemed to have gotten everything from my unconscious mind that had been stored there. Preparations for the mass-production factories were being pushed forward and I began to find myself with more and more time on my hands. Accordingly, I set myself to studying the music, art, literature and history of Kilsona.

Since most of this story has been concerned with the things that happened to me personally, I will now include a brief summary of the history of Kilsona since there may be many who will be more interested in this than in my own personal tragedy.

CHAPTER EIGHTEEN

I HAD ONCE THOUGHT THAT IF I EVER RETURNED TO MY OWN world, I would write a complete history of Kilsona. But since my return has been marked by the charge of murdering my brother, I have neither the time nor the inclination to do this, so that a short version will have to serve.

Once Kilsona had a civilization closely resembling that on earth today. It rested, as does ours, on a foundation of steel and coal, but they had also discovered atomic energy and put it to an even better use than we have. They had three races of men, a dominant race, with all of the special privileges assumed by our own ruling race, an older race which had been supplanted, and a young minority race which was kept from rising by racial prejudice and exploitation. The dominant race was divided into many nations much like our own world.

The power of the nations varied. Sometimes one would be stronger than the others, sometimes another. There were many wars. At the opening of what was the eleventh century to them, the most powerful country was a quite small nation consisting mostly of islands. The name of the nation is impossible to translate, so will call them the "A" islanders.

The A islanders had colonized large tracts of what had formerly been savage country and this accounted for much of their importance. They occupied a large section, geographically, of Kilsona.

The people of this country were not long descended from a race of pirates and so they were still war-like and quick to strike a blow at another country. In fact, even at home they were just as war-like and were constantly having fights and arguments. One thing, however, must be said for them—most of their fighting among themselves was done with fists so that there were few deaths.

For a time, it seemed that these people might soon own or dominate all of Kilsona. Then their star began to wane. In the early days of the machine age, when energy and determination was needed above all, they reigned supreme, but in the later stages they fell behind.

The country that rose to take their place, I shall call the B continent. The people of the country of B were mostly descended from the A islanders who had first colonized the country, but there were other strains in their blood. Their chief characteristic was a sort of mental boldness, a willingness to try new things. They were rather overly proud of this and I gathered that these people were rather too easily fooled by politicians and various leaders who sprang up over night.

Despite the great advances made in both of these countries, the people were far from being happy. There were a few very rich people and millions of poor. Although the leaders of the country daily bragged about being richer than ever before, giving impressive figures of how much they produced of everything, there were millions who were unemployed and who did not have enough to eat. The world struggled from one depression to another, despite a great abundance of everything. There were shoemakers out of work and people without shoes to wear, while tons of leather rotted because it could not be sold at the asking price. Land went out of cultivation because farmers were bankrupt, and food was dumped in the sea because the profit on sales was too small, yet millions starved.

Most of the citizens of Kilsona were too busy with their own particular jobs or troubles to wonder why this was so. There was a class of men who wrote for a living— recorders, they were called—who did think and write about the problems. One of these was a man known by the name of H. Geewells, who said: "Human society has grown up by chance; what is needed is collective planning."

Simple and obvious as this was, it took him all of his life and a hundred books to say it. It was almost the only clear, coherent thought produced in all of this age, yet there were few who were willing even to listen to him.

The simple fact was that humanity on Kilsona had been betrayed by the scientists and the people could not see it. Partly, this was because the scientists had given the people many wonderful things in the way of food, clothing, and means of pleasure—providing the people could afford to buy them—and this fact blinded them to the greater reality that the scientists were also contributing improved ideas on how people could kill each other and methods for a few to hold power over the many. But it was not surprising since many of the scientists were themselves fooled. Although most of them were also poor, they were so pleased by the little attention they got from the military and economic rulers that they blinded themselves to the fact that they had a duty towards an the people.

So the scientists studied dead things, atoms and planets and rocks, and forgot to pay attention to the living. They ignored the fact that the only proper study for man is man.

They learned how to make powerful weapons, but they left the science of running governments, of looking after the people who composed the world, to the hands of politicians. A hundred forms of dangerous experiments were peddled and tried out—one bad one being supplanted by a worse.

One of the chief failures was in the field of psychology, the study of the mind of man. Men lived in constant fear of war and want, but nothing was done to eliminate this. Those few scientists who entered the field of psychology, for the most part, grew as greedy as the overlords and be- came more concerned with removing money from their patients than removing the abreactions that destroyed them. In every way, man was pushed into a mold, which only fitted him for destruction on a grander scale than before.

The climax of the failure of science came in the thirteenth century when a terrible war, much as it had been predicted by H. Geewells in his magnificent book "War from the Clouds," destroyed every large city in Kilsona. Only the small towns and tiny villages were left, without means of communicating with each other. It took hundreds of years for the people to recover from the shock, but even then it was one village against another, tribe against tribe.

This condition continued for hundreds of years. There was little advancement of any kind and the land was filled with suffering. The records of these times are very incomplete. It is not definitely known, for example, where the green ape-men first came from, but it is believed that some scientist after the war played at producing human freaks by using x-rays on the embryos and that the cavemen were the only result that survived.

Thousands of years passed without much change except that the intelligence of the beasts slowly improved while that of the men remained static. Then came a new form of life, clever and malicious—the Larbies. Some historians thought they came from another planet, but it's more probable that they had existed and developed for thousands of years in the mysterious depths of the sea and finally came forth to conquer the land. They were well equipped with the weapons of war and it was not long before they had taken over all of Kilsona, save that small portion inhabited by the men of Gorlem.

The small group of Gorlemites, representing all that was left of the once-proud race of man, had continued to fight against the Larbies and had at least held their own up to the time when I became a resident of Impel.

CHAPTER NINETEEN

MY NEXT FEW YEARS IN IMPEL WERE FAIRLY UNEVENTFUL, although generally I was happy—as happy as a man can be who has been torn from his own world and tossed into another. During this time, Issa bore me three children, two boys and a girl. All were missing the features of the caveman body I occupied, for which I was glad.

Meanwhile, other events were moving swiftly during those five years. Plans for striking a fatal blow in the war were being pushed forward as quickly as possible. Mass production was in existence and I heard rumors that they were using many other things that the scientists had plucked from my unconscious mind. One of the things that I did see was an infrared searchlight, which they had invented, enabling them to see the enemy in the darkness without giving away their own position.

Once mass production was under way, it was known that this would indicate a growing defiance to the Larbies, whose indicators would surely show the vibrations of many machines. There was a mounting tension in all Gorlem.

For weeks there was no reaction, the Larbies seemingly taking no notice of our new activities. But no one was lulled into a sense of false security when the weeks stretched into months. We knew it could only mean that the Larbies were themselves preparing some blow that they hoped would be final.

I was home, listening to recorded music, when the buzzer rang, indicating that I was wanted in one of the science offices. I hurried over and was met by the white-haired scientist who had been my first tutor. I had a feeling that there was something unusual in the air when I saw the expression on his face.

"They are coming, Kastrove," he said calmly.

"The Larbies?" I asked even though I knew the answer.

"Yes, the struggle is about to begin. Three fleets of huge airships have been seen traveling over the desert. From the angle of flight, they apparently plan to meet a few miles north of us. We believe this is meant to be their all-out effort."

"Remember your promise," I reminded him.

"I have not forgotten," he said. "You wanted to be with the defenders at the point where the enemy fleet first touches the Desert of Impel. Judging by the reported movements of the Larbies, this will probably be Defense Post Number 536. There is already a small speed car waiting to take you there. Good luck, Kastrove."

Defense Post Number 536 was situated in a region of tumbled rocks, a wild-looking place in which I doubt I could have found my way without help. My driver took me there safely, hiding the car in the shelter provided, and we walked into the post.

"All correct and at your orders," the commander said as soon as he recognized me as a first class scientist.

"Nonsense," I said. "Consider me no more than an observer and carry on. Have you sighted the enemy yet?"

"Several minutes ago. If you'd care to look through the telescope, you can see them yourself."

It was a double-barreled instrument. Gazing through it, I saw a cluster of dark oval shapes, about a hundred of them, I estimated. At the distance they looked like a group of minnows, but I knew that this was a fleet to fear. But there was something surprising and suddenly I realized what it was. These ships were not invisible and yet the Larbies had the power to make them so. Also they were traveling at a very slow rate of speed. This could only mean that the Larbies were so confident in some new invention that they did not fear the battery of guns below.

In the air about the fleet, as I watched, there appeared bright flashes and I realized the Gorlemites were already firing at them. Then I saw one shell burst brightly against the underside of a ship and I felt a surge of elation. The force of the explosion lifted the rear of the ship, making her nose dip to the ground, but then she righted and settled on an even keel. I was holding my breath, waiting for the ship to crash, when to my surprise the ship continued on as if nothing had happened.

"What is this?" I said. "That shell had no effect on the ship!"

"We've discovered that," the commander said grimly. "They've found some new way of protecting themselves."

I felt a stab of fear. Would this mean that all our work of the past five years would mean nothing? If our guns could not bring down the ships, then it could mean only a matter of time until they destroyed the stations and found a way to penetrate the defenses of Impel.

"Best to say nothing to the men about this," I said to the commander, "or they may lose heart."

"They already know," he said, shrugging his shoulders. "But we shall not shirk our duty. We will fight as long as we live. The news has already been passed on to Impel and the other stations."

Back at the telescope, I saw one ship detach itself from the fleet and nose down to search for the station that was firing at it. Soon it was poised almost directly over that other station, not so far from our own. There was a flash of fire from the ship and sand and powdered rock spouted from the earth below, so huge that it blotted out everything for a minute. Then the ship of the Larbies moved off to join the fleet and there were no bursting shells around them. The station had been completely destroyed with that one blast.

The commander of the post came back into the room where I watched.

"In all matters," he said grimly, "affecting the efficiency of this post, I am in command. You have no authority to countermand any orders that I feel affects the military usefulness of this station. Is that correct?"

I nodded, wondering what he was driving at.

"Very well then," he said. "I consider that your presence here handicaps us in fighting and I order you to retire at once to a safe distance in your car. The presence of a first class scientist makes my men hesitate to take risks. These five men of mine—" they entered at this point— "will escort you to your car. They are instructed to use force if necessary."

Although I wanted to stay, clearly I could not argue with him, so I followed the five men out. But I couldn't help wondering if his orders had come from Impel; that the scientists were trying to give me my way and at the same time frustrate me.

Back in the car, well away from the post, I was startled to see that the enemy was so near that they could be seen by the naked eye. Once again, I watched as one ship left the fleet and destroyed an entire village with one blast.

Clearly, the Larbies had not only new defenses but a new weapon as well.

Bigger and bigger loomed the invading ships, ominous and menacing, seeming to fill the entire sky. The air about us was filled with the thundering roar of their engines. The undersides of the ships gleamed with a green metallic sheen that suggested some new sort of armor plate. And now I could see the shells of the Gorlemites bursting against it without making an impression.

By this time, the invaders were nearing the post that I had just left, and I wondered why the men were withholding their fire. Then I got the answer for suddenly every gun in the post fired at once and I saw that they had all aimed at the same ship. That concentrated fire was too much and to my joy a searing flash of light shot out from the ship. It reared upwards, fluttering like a leaf in the wind, turned over showing its belly to the sun, then shot toward the ground. Above it, the fleet scattered except for one vessel, which swung over toward the post.

Suddenly the whole world rocked around me. It seemed that all of the light was shut out, and then there was a blast of sound that knocked me from my feet. Dust and broken bits of rock swirled around me and rained from the sky. Even before I could see, I knew that the ship had made a direct hit on the post and that only I and my driver were now alive in this section of the desert. We quickly got into our car and secured the windows against the clouds of dust.

As soon as the dust settled, I looked out and saw that my hunch had been right. Where the post had been, the desert was now scooped out like mud by some giant child's spade. Even as we looked, we heard the sound of more explosions farther off and I knew that other posts were falling.

We drove away from them, skirting over the edge of a nearby hill so that we might get a look at the one ship that had been shot down. From the summit, we saw the ship where it had smashed into the land. There were no signs of life around it, and I noticed that the desert around the vessel seemed to be wetted, as though it had rained there.

It was now late in the afternoon and I thought it would be best to wait for the night and make our way back to Impel in the darkness.

That night we slept in our car. Towards morning, we were awakened by a tremendous noise, like a continuous thunder, which was not far away. It seemed to be coming towards us. We started the car and hunted around for a high spot from which we could see what was causing it. Finally we found a place and as we drove up over the top of a dune, we saw a sight such as man had never seen before.

There was a single ship, larger than any of the ones we had seen the day before, about three miles from us. It was a half-mile high, but from it to the ground there stretched a continuous ribbon of orange fire; and wherever that fire touched the ground, the desert *boiled*—liquid rocks splashing high into the air.

It passed far to our left and when it was gone we could see that it had left in its wake a frightful ravine, hundreds of yards deep. They were literally carving up the desert. No underground caverns could withstand that merciless probing for it would create great pressure and strains far below the point where the force reached. It could mean the end of Impel itself.

"How long will it take them to carve up the entire desert?" my driver asked.

"A year," I guessed. "Maybe two—but it's only a matter of time."

It was with heavy heart that we started our car again and headed for Elboaz, which we hoped to find still alive. Finding the way was difficult for the desert had been changed considerably and our compass behaved wildly because of the electric and magnetic forces that had been released.

Several hours later, we arrived at Elboaz and once more found a village geared to fight to death. The fighting will of the Gorlemites was something which never ceased to amaze me—for it was the only thing which had supported them in years of fighting against overwhelming odds. And in the face of what seemed like certain defeat, they had lost none of it.

I wanted to stay at Elboaz and make my final stand with them, but the commander would not permit it and once more I was loaded back into my car and started toward Impel. This time I did not resist the suggestion. I felt that I had to make a contribution somehow and if Impel were the only place where I could fight, then to Impel I would go. I did not think it would be long until the Larbies were there too.

When we arrived at Impel, it seemed to me that the entire population was gathered around the ground entrance to the city. Mechanics bustled around, scientists among them working as hard as they were. I looked for the weapons I expected them to be erecting, but all I could see were a number of harmless-looking searchlights pointing skyward.

One of the first people I saw when we stopped was the white-haired scientist who had been my tutor. He paused to greet me, his grim face shiny with sweat.

"What is to be done?" I cried, leaping from the car. I was anxious to take part in some action, being tired of standing by and watching these people be slaughtered.

"Very little, Kastrove," he said. "We have a new weapon—one based on information you gave us—but we still need a little time to have it ready. Fortunately, the Larbies are still some distance from here."

"Where is the new weapon?" I asked, looking at the searchlights.

"You're looking at it, Kastrove."

"But what is it? A new ray gun?"

"In a way," he said. "It is an ultra-sonics gun."

He hurried off before I could ask more questions and I stood around, feeling as if the whole world had gone mad. I failed to see how those searchlights, despite the fancy name they had given them, could possibly compete with the weapons I had seen the Larbies using. While I was wondering about it, I looked around and then jumped with fear. There was a huge enemy ship, not more than five hundred yards from us and headed directly toward us. I shouted a warning only to be met by grins of amusement.

The white-haired scientist came towards me, his face one broad smile of satisfaction.

"Your ultra-sonic ray is a complete success," he announced. "While you have been standing there, it has brought down three enemy ships and in ten minutes more we shall have two additional projectors in position. I believe the war will soon be won."

"But that ship there—" I said, pointing.

"Everybody aboard is dead. See, it's settling to the ground. Ah, the operators have sighted another ship coming to see what the trouble is… Think you've got it?" he called.

"Think so," shouted the crew around the searchlight. "On the cross-hairs. Heating up now… Yes, the ship seems to be going out of control."

"What's this all about?" I demanded. "You call this thing my ultra-sonic ray—and I don't even know what it's doing."

"It's ultra-sonics," my friend said. "That is ultra-sound. Sound that can't be heard. You told us about it."

I stared at him. I'm sure that my face mirrored the utter blankness that I felt. I failed to see how sound—and sound that couldn't be heard at that—could be such a powerful weapon.

"You told us," he continued, beaming, "that sounds are vibrations in the air, but if these vibrations are faster than 40,000 a second the sound will be on a note too high for the ear to hear."

"Of course."

"Now, quartz is very hard and electric currents can make quartz vibrate very rapidly. Vibrations as fast as 500,000 a second can be produced and projected in a beam. Our searchlight, as you called it, is constructed of quartz.

"If water is subjected to these very rapid vibrations any living things in the water, except bacteria, are killed. The cells of their bodies are torn to pieces. That was all that you told us and we were left to apply it."

"But how?"

"We have always known," he said, "that the Larbies are unable to stay out of water for any length of time. So all of their ships are equipped with tanks of water—in fact, except for the slave ships, they are completely filled with water, so that the Larbies can stay out and fight indefinitely."

I was remembering the wetness I had noticed about the one ship wrecked in the desert. Of course. The Larbies were sea creatures and would have to operate from water. I realized that when I was their slave, I had only seen them out of water for a few minutes at a time.

"So all we had to do," my friend was continuing, "was to perfect a machine which would project the quartz sound waves to their ships. Their armor was no longer any protection."

When the first glow of dawn appeared in the east, a dozen of the death-dealing, innocent-looking machines had been placed in position. It was somehow ghostly to watch them in operation—hearing or seeing nothing, yet knowing that they were sending out vibrations that were killing the Larbies by the hundreds.

All that day our men watched and killed, and all the following week. Then our foes came no more. All in one day, they vanished as if they had never been. Not more than half of their vessels had been brought down, but I think that in some headquarters, perhaps deep beneath the surface of the sea, they realized the power of our new weapon and that the order to retreat had been given.

A few of the ships we brought down had landed without being damaged and the secret of their sciences was ours. With these new additional weapons, it was felt that man never need fear the Larbies again.

It really seemed that the Larbies recognized this too for never again, as long as I lived on Kilsona, did they make an attempt to again enslave man. Indeed, not a single Larby was even seen again.

After I had been ten years on Kilsona, the re-claiming of the desert was well advanced and much of it was irrigated and cultivated again as it had been thousands of years before. Years on that world were twice as long as on ours and I was now of an age equal to forty years, a fairly advanced age for a green man of Graypec. In all, I spent thirty years on Kilsona, but after those first few dangerous years ending with the battle that saved Impel, I settled down to a peaceful and fairly comfortable life.

In happiness and content, surrounded by our offspring, the evening of life began to draw near for Issa and myself. With advancing years I began to think more and more of the world I'd left so long before—the world of paved streets and gasoline fumes, of policemen and fine houses. I thought of my brother, Charlie, and my wife, Mary, and was sad. I who had lived such a full, crowded life on Kilsona longed to return to the other life I had left.

Then Issa died. She reached the end of her normal span of years and passed on. By this time, my friends too were dead and my children were occupied with their own families. Time hung heavily on my hands and my thoughts turned almost constantly to my own world. It was foolish to think of my brother, after all these years, still trying to locate me through his microscope—but think of it I did.

And so I brooded. I was tired of Gorlem, tired of sand and rocks, tired of living in a world where I no longer had a part. At last came a day when I knew I had to make some effort to return to my world, no matter how wild.

My plans were made and I soon got them put into action. A new generation had grown up in Impel, one that looked upon me as one of its heroes, almost a legend. So they were eager to aid me even when they thought my request was madness.

In a carefully selected stretch of the desert, free from drifting sand and where plants would grow if they were watered, I made my new home. Here I sank wells and arranged that they should irrigate irregular stretches of ground forming the letters L.S., hundreds of yards long, and an arrow pointing toward my house. I also had my initials painted on the roof of my house and had a number of hats made, all bearing my initials on top. If Charlie was still looking for me, this might help him find me.

Over two years I lived there alone, waiting and hoping. The only times I ever saw anyone was when parties of sightseers would come by to see the eccentric old man who was already a legend in Impel.

The actual moment when Charlie found me I cannot recall. There came a time when I suddenly felt that I was drowning in some fourth-dimensional mist which I could neither see nor feel. I had a sense of being wrenched out of myself, of a freedom that must have been similar to death. I sank into the grip of this force, which was a vast nothingness, and it seemed that I existed there for ages. Then slowly I began to emerge from it, like coming out of a deep sleep. My head ached as if from a blow.

I opened my eyes and saw myself looking at my brother's laboratory. From object to object my eyes ranged, unable to believe what they saw. But the room was filled with familiar objects and I remembered them all. Once more, I was Learoy Spofforth.

Then I saw my brother peering at me anxiously. My first thought was one of surprise for he had not changed a bit; here I had been gone thirty years, the equivalent of sixty years here on my own world, and Charlie did not look a day older.

"Hello, Charlie," I said, wondering if he could recognize me, aging as I had on Kilsona.

"Thank God," Charlie said and a look of relief came over his face.

I staggered to my feet and was surprised to feel the muscles responding as though young once more. I looked down at my hands and they were the hands of a young man. I was back in my own world and in my own body and was still the same age as when I'd left. It was almost too good to be true, yet true it was. I took several more steps just for the sheer joy of feeling young muscles respond.

"Thank God," my brother was saying again, "that I succeeded. I was doubtful of being able to find you again. It's really fortunate that you thought of marking out your initials so quickly."

"So quickly?" I asked.

"Yes. You were gone only a few minutes—although I suppose it did seem longer to you."

"Charlie," I said hoarsely, trying to grasp what I was hearing, "I spent a whole lifetime on that world! I was an old man when I thought of marking the place with my initials."

"A whole lifetime?" echoed Charlie. He sounded excited. "Then their time must be in relationship to their size, as we see it." He went on talking about what a sensation this would cause in scientific circles.

It seemed to me that his voice was fading and I found myself staring with a sort of morbid fascination at the top of his head. This was the man who had sentenced me to live in another's body. There was a sudden alien thought that it would be so easy to crush the bone of that head and, horrified, I struggled against the thought.

Across the ages I heard the voice of my mate, Issa, telling me that once the scientists of Kilsona had known how to transfer personalities, but that sometimes when they reversed the process there would be a mistake and two personalities would war for possession of one body.

Had the same thing happened to me? All I knew was that I felt drugged, had the impression that some alien strength was lifting my hand and making it curl around some heavy weight.

Then I hardly knew what happened. I felt the primitive surge in me grow stronger and I felt my muscles moving involuntarily. Then there was a blank period in my mind, a blacking out which I welcomed.

I came around to find myself struggling with several men. There was Charlie's butler, a gardener, a policeman, and a stranger, and they were dragging me along the corridor.

"Imagine him killing his own brother," I heard one of them mutter. And then I remembered no more until I found myself in prison, waiting to be charged with the murder of Charlie. It was then that I started writing this story.

More time must have passed since I started this than I realize and I am at a loss to know why they haven't tried me as yet. Obviously, I must be guilty. Yet, for some reason, they seem to have moved me to another building that is unlike most prisons. I'm permitted to walk about on the lawn and I've managed to make two new friends who call to see me quite often. One is a man, who is very friendly, and the other is a beautiful young woman. They both look familiar yet I have no memory of meeting them before. Sometimes, I seem to almost remember them, but then it fades.

Still I am thankful for their friendship since it makes the long wait before my trial less tedious. I can't imagine why they are so friendly unless it's merely that they feel pity for a man who has killed his brother. The woman often cries when she is saying goodbye to me…

EPILOGUE

THE YOUNG WOMAN FINISHED READING THE CLOSELY WRITTEN sheets of paper and placed them on the table. There were tears in her eyes but she blinked them away as she turned to the man who had waited while she read.

"Learoy wrote all of this since he's been in the sanitarium?" she asked.

The man nodded.

"Is it true?" she wanted to know.

"I think so," the man said. "All that we can verify is the very beginning and the end, but I think the rest of it is true. He may have imagined it while he was unconscious after the current was turned on—I suppose that is what science will say. But I will stake my reputation on the fact that he did exchange thoughts, perhaps even souls, with a savage from that atom world."

"You should know," she said, but there was no reproof in her voice.

"I'm sorry, Mary," the man said. He paused, then continued: "There is another reason why I'm sure that Learoy was on Kilsona and lived there for thirty years—by their time."

"What is it?"

"There is nothing else to account for his present condition. But if he grew to be an old man there on that world and then suddenly found himself back in his own body, only thirty years of age, being told that he was gone for only a few minutes, the shock might well unbalance his mind—temporarily."

"You think he will recover?" the young woman asked eagerly.

"Of course. He is all right now except for one thing—and that is his belief that he murdered me."

"But, Charles, why doesn't he recognize us?"

"As the doctor and I have worked it out," Charles Spofforth said, "Learoy's time on Kilsona—or his illusion of being there, as the doctor prefers to think—did two things to him. First, he undoubtedly felt a great hostility towards me, believing that I had sent him there and then abandoned him. Probably, on an unconscious level because he is fond of me, he sometimes wished he could murder me. When he returned, the shock brought on an abreaction so that for a moment that wish returned. All he did was give me a bump over one ear with a small microscope, but the fact that he'd had the wish and had suffered guilt over it made him think that he had killed me. This was helped by the gardener thinking I was dead and making some remark."

"But," said Mary Spofforth, "that doesn't explain why he doesn't recognize us."

"I'm coming to that," the man said. "I don't have to tell you that Learoy was always a sensitive and idealistic man. During the 'thirty years' he was on Kilsona, he mated with the woman Issa who had several children by him, as you've read. But Learoy was always deeply in love with you and so this must have also given him terrible guilt. He now feels that he injured both of us—me by 'murdering' me and you by his infidelity. His guilt makes him refuse to recognize us because then he would have to face his guilt. But the doctor believes that we can soon pull him out of it."

"It seems impossible," she muttered, "that he could have been on that world and did all the things he described."

"You won't let the story of Issa hurt you, will you?" Charles Spofforth asked anxiously. "I know that it may be difficult to accept that Learoy loves you when there was such an infidelity, but you must admit the circumstances were unusual."

"They always are," Mary said with a smile. "No, Charles, I don't even consider that Learoy was unfaithful to me. It wasn't his own body that he used when he slept with her, but that of the ape-man Kastrove. So of course it doesn't count."

It was a logic which hadn't occurred to Charles Spofforth, but if it were the thing to make her forget about Issa, then that was all that was necessary.

"Come," he said. "It's time we started for the sanitarium. The doctor thinks that the more often we see Learoy, the quicker he'll pull through."

"And the quicker he'll forget that Issa," Mary said, rising. "I'll see to that." There was a note in her voice that made Charles realize that she would and gave a pretty clear picture of the method she'd use. Women made their men forget, he reflected as he followed her out of the room, pretty much the same in England as on Kilsona.

THE END

If you've enjoyed this book, you will not want to miss these terrific titles…

ARMCHAIR SCI-FI & HORROR DOUBLE NOVELS, $12.95 each

D-31 **A HOAX IN TIME** by Keith Laumer
INSIDE EARTH by Poul Anderson

D-32 **TERROR STATION** by Dwight V. Swain
THE WEAPON FROM ETERNITY by Dwight V. Swain

D-33 **THE SHIP FROM INFINITY** by Edmond Hamilton
TAKEOFF by C. M. Kornbluth

D-34 **THE METAL DOOM** by David H. Keller
TWELVE TIMES ZERO by Howard Browne

D-35 **HUNTERS OUT OF SPACE** by Joseph Kelleam
INVASION FROM THE DEEP by Paul W. Fairman,

D-36 **THE BEES OF DEATH** by Robert Moore Williams
A PLAGUE OF PYTHONS by Frederick Pohl

D-37 **THE LORDS OF QUARMALL** by Fritz Leiber and Harry Fischer
BEACON TO ELSEWHERE by James H. Schmitz

D-38 **BEYOND PLUTO** by John S. Campbell
ARTERY OF FIRE by Thomas N. Scortia

D-39 **SPECIAL DELIVERY** by Kris Neville
NO TIME FOR TOFFEE by Charles F. Meyers

D-40 **JUNGLE IN THE SKY** by Milton Lesser
RECALLED TO LIFE by Robert Silverberg

ARMCHAIR SCIENCE FICTION CLASSICS, $12.95 each

C-10 **MARS IS MY DESTINATION**
by Frank Belknap Long

C-11 **SPACE PLAGUE**
by George O. Smith

C-12 **SO SHALL YE REAP**
by Rog Phillips

ARMCHAIR SCIENCE FICTION & HORROR GEMS SERIES, $12.95 each

G-3 **SCIENCE FICTION GEMS, Vol. Two**
James Blish and others

G-4 **HORROR GEMS, Vol. Two**
Joseph Payne Brennan and others

If you've enjoyed this book, you will not want to miss these terrific titles…

ARMCHAIR SCI-FI, FANTASY, & HORROR DOUBLE NOVELS, $12.95 each

D-41 **FULL CYCLE** by Clifford D. Simak
IT WAS THE DAY OF THE ROBOT by Frank Belknap Long

D-42 **THIS CROWDED EARTH** by Robert Bloch
REIGN OF THE TELEPUPPETS by Daniel Galouye

D-43 **THE CRISPIN AFFAIR** by Jack Sharkey
THE RED HELL OF JUPITER by Paul Ernst

D-44 **PLANET OF DREAD** by Dwight V. Swain
WE THE MACHINE by Gerald Vance

D-45 **THE STAR HUNTER** by Edmond Hamilton
THE ALIEN by Raymond F. Jones

D-46 **WORLD OF IF** by Rog Phillips
SLAVE RAIDERS FROM MERCURY by Don Wilcox

D-47 **THE ULTIMATE PERIL** by Robert Abernathy
PLANET OF SHAME by Bruce Elliot

D-48 **THE FLYING EYES** by J. Hunter Holly
SOME FABULOUS YONDER by Phillip Jose Farmer

D-49 **THE COSMIC BUNGLERS** by Geoff St. Reynard
THE BUTTONED SKY by Geoff St. Reynard

D-50 **TYRANTS OF TIME** by Milton Lesser
PARIAH PLANET by Murray Leinster

ARMCHAIR SCIENCE FICTION CLASSICS, $12.95 each

C-13 **SUNKEN WORLD**
by Stanton A. Coblentz

C-14 **THE LAST VIAL**
by Sam McClatchie, M. D.

C-15 **WE WHO SURVIVED (THE FIFTH ICE AGE)**
by Sterling Noel

ARMCHAIR MASTERS OF SCIENCE FICTION SERIES, $16.95 each

MS-5 **MASTERS OF SCIENCE FICTION, Vol. Five**
Winston K. Marks—Test Colony and other tales

MS-6 **MASTERS OF SCIENCE FICTION, Vol. Six**
Fritz Leiber—Deadly Moon and other tales

If you've enjoyed this book, you will not want to miss these terrific titles…

ARMCHAIR SCI-FI & HORROR DOUBLE NOVELS, $12.95 each

D-51 **A GOD NAMED SMITH** by Henry Slesar
WORLDS OF THE IMPERIUM by Keith Laumer

D-52 **CRAIG'S BOOK** by Don Wilcox
EDGE OF THE KNIFE by H. Beam Piper

D-53 **THE SHINING CITY** by Rona M. Vale
THE RED PLANET by Russ Winterbotham

D-54 **THE MAN WHO LIVED TWICE** by Rog Phillips
VALLEY OF THE CROEN by Lee Tarbell

D-55 **OPERATION DISASTER** by Milton Lesser
LAND OF THE DAMNED by Berkeley Livingston

D-56 **CAPTIVE OF THE CENTAURIANESS** by Poul Anderson
A PRINCESS OF MARS by Edgar Rice Burroughs

D-57 **THE NON-STATISTICAL MAN** by Raymond F. Jones
MISSION FROM MARS by Rick Conroy

D-58 **INTRUDERS FROM THE STARS** by Ross Rocklynne
FLIGHT OF THE STARLING by Chester S. Geier

D-59 **COSMIC SABOTEUR** by Frank M. Robinson
LOOK TO THE STARS by Willard Hawkins

D-60 **THE MOON IS HELL!** by John W. Campbell, Jr.
THE GREEN WORLD by Hal Clement

ARMCHAIR SCIENCE FICTION CLASSICS, $12.95 each

C-16 **THE SHAVER MYSTERY, Book Three**
by Richard S. Shaver

C-17 **THE PLANET STRAPPERS**
by Raymond Z. Gallun

C-18 **THE FOURTH "R"**
by George O. Smith

ARMCHAIR SCIENCE FICTION & HORROR GEMS SERIES, $12.95 each

G-5 **SCIENCE FICTION GEMS, Vol. Three**
C. M. Kornbluth and others

G-6 **HORROR GEMS, Vol. Three**
August Derleth and others

If you've enjoyed this book, you will not want to miss these terrific titles…

ARMCHAIR SCI-FI & HORROR DOUBLE NOVELS, $12.95 each

D-61   **THE MAN WHO STOPPED AT NOTHING** by Paul W. Fairman
TEN FROM INFINITY by Ivar Jorgensen

D-62   **WORLDS WITHIN** by Rog Phillips
THE SLAVE by C.M. Kornbluth

D-63   **SECRET OF THE BLACK PLANET** by Milton Lesser
THE OUTCASTS OF SOLAR III by Emmett McDowell

D-64   **WEB OF THE WORLDS** by Harry Harrison and Katherine MacLean
RULE GOLDEN by Damon Knight

D-65   **TEN TO THE STARS** by Raymond Z. Gallun
THE CONQUERORS by David H. Keller, M. D.

D-66   **THE HORDE FROM INFINITY** by Dwight V. Swain
THE DAY THE EARTH FROZE by Gerald Hatch

D-67   **THE WAR OF THE WORLDS** by H. G. Wells
THE TIME MACHINE by H. G. Wells

D-68   **STARCOMBERS** by Edmond Hamilton
THE YEAR WHEN STARDUST FELL by Raymond F. Jones

D-69   **HOCUS-POCUS UNIVERSE** by Jack Williamson
QUEEN OF THE PANTHER WORLD by Berkeley Livingston

D-70   **BATTERING RAMS OF SPACE** by Don Wilcox
DOOMSDAY WING by George H. Smith

ARMCHAIR SCIENCE FICTION & FANTASY CLASSICS, $12.95 each

C-19   **EMPIRE OF JEGGA**
by David V. Reed

C-20   **THE TOMORROW PEOPLE**
by Judith Merril

C-21   **THE MAN FROM YESTERDAY**
by Howard Browne as by Lee Francis

C-22   **THE TIME TRADERS**
by Andre Norton

C-23   **ISLANDS OF SPACE**
by John W. Campbell

C-24   **THE GALAXY PRIMES**
by E. E. "Doc" Smith

If you've enjoyed this book, you will not want to miss these terrific titles…

ARMCHAIR SCI-FI & HORROR DOUBLE NOVELS, $12.95 each

D-71 **THE DEEP END** by Gregory Luce
       TO WATCH BY NIGHT by Robert Moore Williams

D-72 **SWORDSMAN OF LOST TERRA** by Poul Anderson
       PLANET OF GHOSTS by David V. Reed

D-73 **MOON OF BATTLE** by J. J. Allerton
       THE MUTANT WEAPON by Murray Leinster

D-74 **OLD SPACEMEN NEVER DIE!** John Jakes
       RETURN TO EARTH by Bryan Berry

D-75 **THE THING FROM UNDERNEATH** by Milton Lesser
       OPERATION INTERSTELLAR by George O. Smith

D-76 **THE BURNING WORLD** by Algis Budrys
       FOREVER IS TOO LONG by Chester S. Geier

D-77 **THE COSMIC JUNKMAN** by Rog Phillips
       THE ULTIMATE WEAPON by John W. Campbell

D-78 **THE TIES OF EARTH** by James H. Schmitz
       CUE FOR QUIET by Thomas L. Sherred

D-79 **SECRET OF THE MARTIANS** by Paul W. Fairman
       THE VARIABLE MAN by Philip K. Dick

D-80 **THE GREEN GIRL** by Jack Williamson
       THE ROBOT PERIL by Don Wilcox

ARMCHAIR SCIENCE FICTION CLASSICS, $12.95 each

C-25 **THE STAR KINGS**
  b   y Edmond Hamilton

C-26 **NOT IN SOLITUDE**
       by Kenneth Gantz

C-32 **PROMETHEUS II**
       by S. J. Byrne

ARMCHAIR SCIENCE FICTION & HORROR GEMS SERIES, $12.95 each

G-7 **SCIENCE FICTION GEMS, Vol. Seven**
      Jack Sharkey and others

G-8 **HORROR GEMS, Vol. Eight**
      Seabury Quinn and others

If you've enjoyed this book, you will not want to miss these terrific titles…

ARMCHAIR SCI-FI, FANTASY, & HORROR DOUBLE NOVELS, $12.95 each

D-81   **THE LAST PLEA** by Robert Bloch
OMEGA by Robert Sheckley

D-82   **WOMAN FROM ANOTHER PLANET** by Frank Belknap Long
HOMECALLING by Judith Merril

D-83   **WHEN TWO WORLDS MEET** by Robert Moore Williams
THE MAN WHO HAD NO BRAINS by Jeff Sutton

D-84   **THE SPECTRE OF SUICIDE SWAMP** by E. K. Jarvis
IT'S MAGIC, YOU DOPE! by Jack Sharkey

D-85   **THE STARSHIP FROM SIRIUS** by Rog Phillips
FINAL WEAPON by Everett Cole

D-86   **TREASURE ON THUNDER MOON** by Edmond Hamilton
TRAIL OF THE ASTROGAR by Henry Haase

D-87   **THE VENUS ENIGMA** by Joe Gibson
THE WOMAN IN SKIN 13 by Paul W. Fairman

D-88   **THE MAD ROBOT** by William P. McGivern
THE RUNNING MAN by J. Holly Hunter

D-89   **VENGEANCE OF KYVOR** by Randall Garrett
AT THE EARTH'S CORE by Edgar Rice Burroughs

D-90   **DWELLERS OF THE DEEP** by Don Wilcox
NIGHT OF THE LONG KNIVES by Fritz Leiber

ARMCHAIR SCIENCE FICTION CLASSICS, $12.95 each

C-28   **THE MAN FROM TOMORROW**
by Stanton A. Coblentz

C-29   **THE GREEN MAN OF GRAYPEC**
by Festus Pragnell

C-30   **THE SHAVER MYSTERY, Book Four**
by Richard S. Shaver

ARMCHAIR MASTERS OF SCIENCE FICTION SERIES, $16.95 each

MS-7   **MASTERS OF SCIENCE FICTION AND FANTASY, Vol. Seven**
Lester del Rey, "The Band Played on" and other tales

MS-8   **MASTERS OF SCIENCE FICTION, Vol. Eight**
Milton Lesser, "'A' is for Android" and other tales